Monster
on the
Moors

A Bobby Holmes Mystery

Monster on the Moors

A Bobby Holmes Mystery

by

J. M. Kelly

Top Publications, Ltd.

Monster on the Moors
A Bobby Holmes Mystery
Volume 2

© COPYRIGHT
J. M. Kelly
2019

Top Publications, Ltd.
Plano, Texas

Paperback Edition
ISBN 978-1-7333283-6-4

Acknowledgments

Inspiration comes from many sources, and the major muse for this novel is the landscape. The North York Moors is a hauntingly beautiful place, one I highly recommend visiting. It has stirred the creative juices of Bram Stoker (Dracula), Sir Arthur Conan Doyle (Hound of the Baskervilles), and James Herriot (All Creatures Great and Small). From the small village of Goathland, to the windswept escarpments of Whitby, I simply couldn't resist its lure and stimulus.

Once again, I am indebted to Kendall Spangler for her artistic genius in creating the cover for my novel. One look at it compels me to open and read, the goal of every author.

I extend my deepest thanks to Helga Schier, withpenandpaper.com, for her expert guidance in editing, constructive criticism, and everything it takes to render a final copy. She simply makes me a better writer, and her efforts are greatly appreciated.

And, lastly, to my biggest fan base, Peter, Alex, Brianna, and my greatest supporter, my wife Bronwen.

1

The wind stroked his matted fur, tugging at him with probing fingers as he raced across the dampened field. Burrs hitched a ride on his hindquarters, while a flattened path of purple heather followed his trace over the windblown hilltop. Saliva careened down his chin and caressed his puffing cheeks. He was hungry and he was on the hunt.

He scurried down a gentle knoll where he paused, then sprinted up a small slope. His torn clothes snapped in the breeze, the only sound to be heard on this cool evening, aside from his rapid breathing. He reached the crest of the ridge as the moon pierced the clouds, lighting the landscape before him. He gazed up for a moment, eyes wide in wonder. He tilted his head back, bared his massive incisors and let out a howl so terrifying no animal dared to answer it.

The moon's glow bounced off his glistening eyes. He curled his clawed hands tightly, then slowly released them. He sniffed to pick up the rapidly vanishing scent he chased. He breathed in the sweat and fear that faintly lingered there, savoring its promise, turned his head to the left and sped towards the darkened forest below.

The vegetation grew thicker here. There were heavily rooted trees of oak and ash, as well as fragrant thickets of pine and low brush. The air was thicker too, as the surrounding peaks cut the fast-moving wind to a crawl. The evening dew hung by a finger from the bending leaves and branches, falling quietly to the soft earth below. He stopped at a clearing.

His prey was close. This would no longer be a hunt. It would be a slaughter.

He heard the soft patter of rapidly moving footsteps to his right. His superior peripheral and night vision allowed him to catch a brief glimpse of the female he stalked, as she fearfully scampered through the blackened forest. He snarled, saliva now flowing in anticipation of the imminent meal. He loped through the congested trees, his breath arriving split seconds before him in the chilled night air. He taunted his victim, growling his location every few feet. The head of the poor woman swiveled with each guttural sound, trying to pinpoint the location of her stalker, letting out an uncontrolled screech each time she heard him. She breathed rapidly and scuttled backwards, her darting eyes trying to anticipate the direction of the attack. Finally, she tripped and fell, and pressed her back against a sturdy oak.

It was time. The beast sauntered into the small clearing, facing his prey. He stood there, still and silent, waiting for his quarry to notice him. When she did, the creature stood up on his hind legs to his full seven-foot height. He bared his fangs, unfurled his

"With my old friend Sally Jenkins. I haven't seen her in years. She runs a Bed and Breakfast called the Wolf's Head Inn, in the small town of Goathland."

The Moors was an area reminiscent of old Britain: a National Park of mysterious rolling hills, eye-popping color from the yearly heather that grew across it, woodlands that spoke in whispers they were so old, and, at times, an eerie silence that simply kept one in awe. Bobby had visited the area once as a child and had never forgotten the way the natural splendor had assaulted his senses.

"You're smiling again!" said his mum.

"I can't help it. I'm so looking forward to this holiday. I know it's only a two-hour train ride to York, but I just can't wait."

"Don't get ahead of yourself, Bobby. Once in York, we still have at least an hour of car time to get to Goathland, and Brenda and your friends won't be arriving until tomorrow. So, do try and relax."

Bobby went back to staring out the window. He drifted into a sleepy haze, his eyelids drooping and his smile fading. The gentle rocking of the train nudged him into a light slumber, with visions of hiking through the forest playing on the edge of awareness.

He was in the forest with his mates. Things smelled warm and moist, like newly spaded earth. Clods of dark dirt flipped up behind them as they walked, churned by the sturdy hiking shoes they wore. The sun filtered through the overhanging brush, tagging them with fingers of light. He could hear the soft crush of leaves underfoot, and the gentle rustle of branches caused by the calm wind that cooled him with each step. He felt good. And calm, as if this was where he was supposed to be, accompanied by those he most treasured. Suddenly, and without warning, the sun hid behind a dark cloud and night descended like a silent curtain, as if the lights had been switched off in the forest. They paused in their travels, senses on full alert, realizing that one of them was missing. No moon shone through the interlocking branches. A gust of wind suddenly blew through and around them and they huddled against the biting cold. Bobby could hear his comrades whisper but couldn't discern what they said. The dark cloud moved, as if by a heavy hand, and moonlight flooded the forest, showering their band in a white, bright glow. Dead silence rained on them. Nothing could be heard but their hurried breaths and the relentless ticking of Bobby's wristwatch. Suddenly a loud, soul crushing howl pierced the night, coming from every angle at once, blanketing the darkened forest with its frightening portent...

Bobby awoke.

The train let out a second howl, and Bobby's mum announced they were nearing their stop. Bobby shook his head to clear the fading vision and gathered his belongings. The train's pace was ramped back by the engineer, and the houses they passed took on more definition, gradually losing the blur that occurs by passing a stationary object at great speed. It took a few minutes, but soon the station sign loomed bearing the name of their destination: York. When the train came to a full stop on Platform 11, Bobby and his mum had an emblem entitled The Goathland Wolf's Head Inn across the left breast. He stood a little over five feet tall, had a long, thick nose and was as wide as he was tall. His voice was gruff, and Bobby thought he resembled the picture of a troll he had seen in a book recently.

"Well hello, then," she said. "Indeed, I'm Melanie Holmes and this is my son Bobby. Thank you for coming to pick us up, today."

"My pleasure, Miss." He tipped his cap and looked at Bobby. It was a strange look, one that held Bobby's eyes a moment longer than was necessary. Bobby felt slightly uncomfortable. Then, quickly, the strange little man bent to pick up their bags and said, "Follow me please."

Their guide waddle-walked across the wide platform, balanced with their two medium sized suitcases and led them to the nearby car park, their unpleasant experience in the tunnel now disappearing into a foggy memory soon to be forgotten.

"Why are there so many sheep?" asked Bobby, careful not to misstep.

"Because there are still many farmers up here in the moors. Lots of grazing about. You'll notice that the sheep have a dash of color spray painted on their bottom. That's to identify the owners. If any get lost or wander off too far, we'll know they belong to."

Bobby couldn't help but stare at the fluffy beasts, chewing away with abandon, sporting a spot of bright color on their hindquarters. The town itself was much smaller than Bobby had imagined. Aside from a handful of inns and B&Bs, there were only a few small shops—a shoe repair, a curiosity shop, a confectionary and the like—along with several patches of open greens, all now filled with hungry sheep. It didn't take long, therefore, to reach the Wolf's Head Inn, located on the southern edge of town, near the street called Two Howes Pass. The inn was made of limestone, which glowed in the setting sun. It was perhaps the tallest building in Goathland, save the church, which branched off to the left, along the same path that led to the Wolf's Head Inn.

The inn was an imposing edifice. It had four chimneys, three large bay windows across the front, along with three dormers peeking out of the gabled rooftop. Its roof was made of slate shingles, some of them covered with wet, shiny green moss. Flower boxes, filled with a riot of colorful Asters, underpinned every window, and the oversized entry was crowned with an equally large wooden sign. The sign hung perpendicular to the inn on two well-anchored, wrought iron hinges. It was a five foot by three-foot piece of old timber that local rumor attributed to a two hundred year old sailing vessel out of Whitby. There was no mistaking that the sign could withstand any foul weather Mother Nature intended, and Mother Nature could indeed be harsh on the moors. The inn's name was painted in gold, in a half-circle spanning the antique frontispiece in Old-English font. And just below the name was a large, carnivorous wolf's head, saliva dripping from the massive fangs protruding from its powerful jaw.

"Oh, my," said Melanie.

"Kind of takes your breath away when you first see it, don't it Miss?"

"Yes, James, it certainly does. I assume it has a different...ah, feel, inside?"

"Why, yes, Miss Melanie, Miss Sally has indeed put her touch to the test on the interior, to be sure. I do believe you'll find it quite welcoming."

James pushed open the massive portals and they drifted through the gaping maw, as the sun waned behind them. They took tentative steps forward until their eyes could adjust to the darkened interior, glancing about with dilated pupils. James flicked a light switch and they couldn't help but be surprised. There were large curtains on every window, and expensive area rugs that defined a multitude of spaces for gathering. The walls were painted a soft white, reflecting the warm glow of the many table lamps. Prints of impressionist paintings, scenes of calm lakes, peaceful streets, and radiant gardens graced the walls, probably take that challenge," James calmly responded.

Brenda rolled her eyes, knowing that Stevie hated not having the last word. "Come on," she said, grabbing his arm. "Let's go explore the train and see if we can get something to drink."

"Not to worry, Miss Brenda, they'll bring a cart around with refreshments, shortly," offered James. Everyone settled into their seats and watched the countryside whizzing past in a glorious mélange of color.

Time swiftly passed with other, less volatile topics discussed. James loved to talk, especially about the history of his country. With a captive audience, he went on for some time, and Bobby and his friends were drawn in by the colorful stories of knights and warfare. He also loved to play tour guide.

"Now see here, everyone," said James, trying to get their attention. "Whitby is an exciting, bustling and beautiful seaside town, nestled on the edge of the North Yorkshire coast, where the River Esk meets the North Sea. At the mouth of the river, two massive man-made breakers guide ships into port, like two pincers feeding a hungry crab." James demonstrated with his hands. "The bay is flanked by two massive cliffs," he continued. "The West cliff sports a dedication to Whitby's famous maritime hero, Captain Cook, as well as the noted Whalebone Arch, commemorating Whitby's historical connection to the whaling industry." Bobby and Brenda were listening, Michael leaned over the back of the seat occupied by James, while Stevie was distracted by nearly everyone and everything. "The prominent feature of the East cliff is St. Mary's church and the ruins of Whitby Abbey. The East Cliff may be approached by road from the church or by climbing the one hundred and ninety-nine steps known as the Church Stairs."

"Hey we're here!" shouted Stevie.

The train jolted to a dead stop, nearly jostling the passengers off their seats. Stevie was the first one to the exit, wanting to leap from the top step. As he was about to get airborne, James reached out and grabbed him by the scruff of the neck.

"Hold on there, young master. I need to secure us a map and a few guide brochures from the office. You need to take these steps one at a time and then sit over there on that bench until I get back. Are we clear?"

"Of course, my good man, whatever you say," uttered Stevie, sarcasm dripping from his lips.

James slowly turned towards Stevie. He glared for a moment, before saying, "And you need to stop calling me 'my good man.' Would that be alright with you?"

"Of course, my goo…Oops. Ah, no problem, James. You can count on me" Stevie rolled his eyes.

"Yes, I'm sure I can," said James, shaking his head as he proceeded towards the office.

Bobby hung back for a moment, while Brenda and Michael gathered their things. He glanced out the window and now clearly saw the waiter from Goathland scurrying along the platform. He had the same dark hair parted in the middle, a cigarette dangling from his lips, and his shirt sleeves rolled up. He was moving in a hurry, with the same look of quiet intensity on his face. Bobby raced along the train car, looking out the window, staring at the man, a sense of dread rising inside of him, until he could go no further. He stuck his head out the door exit just to catch the waiter rounding the corner of the station house. He paused, a barrage of images racing in his head. Brenda moved up behind him.

"What's wrong?" she asked.

"I don't have time to explain, right now. I need to follow someone. Tell James. I think he'll understand. I'll find you all later or meet you back here at the station at 5:00. I promise I'll explain when we meet." He leaped off the train in hot pursuit. Brenda yelled, "Bobby, wait," but he was already turning the corner and didn't even slow down.

"Hey, where's he going," yelled Stevie, now up from the bench.

"I'm not sure," Brenda said. "He saw someone get off the train and he ran after him. Listen Stevie," she added, "he looked frightened."

"I know," countered Stevie. "He told me we were in some kind of trouble and he'd explain later. I'm going after him!"

"Oh no you're not," said Brenda. But before she could finish, Stevie was running in Bobby's direction at full tilt.

"Ugh!"

By that time, Michael had joined her, wondering where everyone was. Brenda turned her head, trying to decide what she should do, when James emerged from the office.

"Now," he said with a broad, cheery smile, "we can proceed towards the swing bridge and from there get a view of the town." He picked his head up from an opened brochure, his face descending into a blank stare. "Where is everyone?"

Michael shrugged his shoulders and Brenda tried to explain. When she relayed what Bobby had said, she noticed that James' right hand began to tremble.

6

J ames stared at Brenda and Michael and, for a split second, contemplated sending them back home on the train. "Follow me," he finally said.

On the other side of the station house, James scanned the area, looking for a young person running. A throng of tourists cluttered the roads and walkways, so it wasn't an easy task, but he soon spotted Stevie darting across a busy street against the light. Once on the other side, Stevie weaved in and out of thick pedestrian traffic, heading in the direction of the swing bridge.

"Stevie!" James shouted, and Brenda and Michael chimed in, but to no avail. Stevie couldn't possibly hear them at this distance. There was only one thing to do. They hurried after him as quickly as they could.

By the time they reached the bridge it was too late. Stevie had scurried across the bridge just before it was closed off to the public, while it swung open parallel to the shore to allow ships to pass. Stevie would now have a substantial lead on them, and they'd have some distance to make up once on the other side. The ten-minute wait was infuriating, but they could do nothing about it. James looked about, seeking an alternative way across, but there was none. Brenda and Michael looked at each other, remembering the horror they'd faced last year, neither anxious to repeat it. Brenda reached out and patted Michael on the shoulder. "It'll be okay, Michael, we'll find them."

The good news was that there was only one destination Stevie and Bobby could possibly be taking: towards the ruins of the 13th century Whitby Abbey at the top of the eastern escarpment. When the bridge finally swung back into place, and they were allowed to cross, dozens of people were trying to cross at once. They had to negotiate their way around the late summer tourists, who were taking their time as they were taking in the sights, increasing their delay.

They made their way through the cobble stoned village streets, crowded with visitors, and elbowed their way over to the Church Stairs, apologizing to those they bumped into. Michael kept his head low and Brenda, holding on to his arm, led him through the thick of it. He detested crowds.

They paused for a brief moment at the base of the 200-year-old flight of stone steps that wound their way up the hillside. James looked nervous, angry, and fearful, as he gaped at the steep stairway, worried about what might have happened to Bobby and Stevie. The ninety-nine worn stairs, bowed in the middle from centuries of use, formed a long, winding climb up the side of the hill. Michael put his arm around James, pointed at the sky, and said, "Don't worry, James, we can make it." James drew in a deep breath, and bolstered by Michael's supportive comment, began a steady, but rapid pace upwards, driven by the guilt of losing two youngsters in his care and by the fear of what might have happened to them. He was soon followed by Brenda and Michael, both of whom struggled to keep up with the much older James.

Bobby was breathing heavily and sweating when he reached the top of the stairs. The weather had turned slightly, bringing a bracing wind that chilled him as he crossed the open field. Before him lay the ruins. Tall and majestic, the skeletal remains of the Abbey looked eerie, as a sudden fog weaved its way through the open arches of the ancient church. The sun was hiding behind darkening clouds, a sole, piercing shaft of light shooting through the church nave like a javelin of fire. There was a smattering of tourists nearby, most exploring the far side of the Abbey, while Bobby meandered through the graveyard alone. The tilted headstones fanned out across the area like crooked teeth. The wind whipped its way around them, and Bobby drew up his collar, wishing he had brought his jacket. He shivered from the cold, damp air, but he shook from something else as well. He knew that the man he chased from the station was here and he was hiding. Bobby could feel it, and the strange snapshots in his head confirmed it.

Bobby drifted among the gravestones. He understood instinctively why this location had inspired Bram Stoker's infamous vampire, Dracula. Where the graves parted, he could see the silhouette of the Abbey, darkened by the dimmed, backlit ray of sunlight. They were soon surrounded by the fog now climbing down the slope towards him. Headstones gathered, leaning on each other for support, refusing to fall due to their age and the effect of the elements. Bobby could not see over or around them, and wherever he could peer between some, others behind them blocked a clear view. The overall effect was claustrophobic. Unknown forces seemed to deliberately box him in. Fog gathered about his ankles. Time stood still. Noise diminished; even the crickets stopped their incessant singing. Bobby sensed that he was in trouble. Before he could turn around, a strong hand fell upon his shoulder. Bobby couldn't move, the grip was so strong. He felt the tingle of hot breath on the back of his ear. The figure leaned forward and slowly whispered.

"I am not what you make of me. Whatever truth you know, or think you know, you have no idea what pain lies in wait for you if you continue to pursue this course. Leave this place and leave me alone to do my work. Do not follow me again. Now, sleep."

Stevie, at last, reached the top step. He had no idea where Bobby had gone and saw no sign to indicate what he should do. Cool, damp air pushed his hair, drying his sweat and giving him goosebumps. He started to panic, when he saw a tall, dark figure jogging towards the Abbey, away from the gravestones that dotted the hillside. Instinct told him Bobby was in trouble. Stevie ran for the headstones. He reached into his pocket and pulled out a few rounded stones, carefully selected for throwing in case he needed protection. He was out of breath when he reached the graveyard but could not stop his frantic search. He feared that Bobby had been attacked and lay injured and helpless among the ancient dead. Fear demanded caution, but with his friend in danger, Stevie could not slow down. He raced among the headstones looking left and right, calling out Bobby's name; silently at first, mostly out of fear, but then ever more loudly in growing desperation. Panic soon overtook him.

Even though he was older, James reached the top first and stopped. Brenda and Michael nearly bumped into him on their ascent. All three scanned the area and saw no sign of their comrades.

"Follow me!" James bellowed, and raced towards the skeletal remains of the Abbey.

When Bobby was much younger, he had been taken to the hospital for a head injury he had sustained falling out of a tree. It gave him a nasty bump on his forehead. They had kept him overnight and his mother insisted on sleeping in the room with him. She wanted to be there when he roused and tend to his needs as only a mother could. Bobby slept deeply that night, barely even dreaming. When he awoke the next morning, it was in stages, as if he were climbing out of a deep, dank cellar, one plodding step at a time. Before he could open his eyes, he was able to hear the mounting morning noise. He heard the nurses stirring, the muted conversations and the low background sounds of the morning news on the tele, blaring banalities at no one in particular. He was tingly and slowly came to life with needles and pins from head to toe.

He felt that way now, as he lay in the open field. He could smell the grass, feel the rough texture of the ground beneath him and hear a distant voice calling his name. At first, he wasn't able to respond. It was much too difficult to try. He was not uncomfortable, but it required a great deal of effort to shout out and he felt too calm to do so. But the voice was insistent. Bobby's eyes flickered. He was able to force one of them open and see that he had been gently placed a few feet from where he had been standing, when...that's right! His memory finally clicked, and he remembered his encounter with the stranger. He forced himself to open his eyes and sit up. A wave of dizziness overtook him. He rubbed an area between his neck and right shoulder. He recalled being squeezed tightly there. After that, he had passed out and descended into darkness.

The voice got louder and the cries more anxious. The pain in his shoulder dissipated.

"Over here!" he hoarsely shouted.

Stevie paused, gauging the direction of the weak cry he heard. He pinpointed the spot and darted over. Peering around a collection of jumbled grave markers, Stevie saw Bobby sitting on a small hill, rubbing his neck. Stevie crouched, eyes darting, poised with one of his rounded stones, ready to throw at a moment's provocation.

James, Brenda, and Michael sprinted through the Abbey ruins, eyes alert, scanning every nook and cranny for Stevie and Bobby. Tourists dotted the interior in small groups, some reading their guidebooks, some being led by a guide who lectured on about the history of the place, while others were just lounging, enjoying the day and resting from the climb to the top of the cliff. Brenda caught sight of a couple standing in a shaded corner of the Abbey, bent over in agitated conversation. From a distance, it appeared to be a monk in a dark hooded robe engaging a tall, dark-haired man in a white shirt with his shirtsleeves rolled up. The monk was moving his arms and waving his hands, enhancing his argument by punching one closed fist into the opened palm of the other hand. The tall man shook his head vigorously and repeatedly jabbed his index finger into the chest of the monk. Brenda moved closer, distancing herself from James and Michael, who were hurriedly moving towards the far end of the remains. She gazed around the Abbey trying to appear disinterested in the conversation of these two men. As she drew nearer, the conversation grew more frantic. She heard the man yell, "I won't stop and I will succeed, with or without you!" He then stormed past Brenda on his hurried way out of the Abbey.

✢✢✢✢✢

Stevie helped Bobby stand up on wonky legs.

"Where is everyone else?" Bobby asked.

"I'm afraid I took off before they did, once I heard you went after someone," Stevie replied.

Bobby shook his head and put his hand on Stevie's shoulder. "Thanks, Stevie," he said with genuine conviction, "I know I can always count on you."

"Hey, I owe you from last year. What now?" Stevie asked.

"I'm not sure if the person I encountered here is friend or foe. I'll have to think about that. Right now, we should look for the others. I'm sure they'll be worried."

"We should go over to the Abbey," Stevie said. "I mean, they're not here, so if James and the others followed me where else would they be?"

As they approached the ancient church, James, Michael, and Brenda jetted out the east end. They caught sight of Bobby and Stevie walking up the hill towards the Abbey and hurried over to them.

"Where have you been?" shouted James at Bobby. "And what were you thinking taking off like that?" he directed at Stevie. "Do you have any idea how much you both worried me? And what will your mother say, Bobby, when I inform her of your irresponsible behavior?"

"Now see here, my good man..." interjected Stevie.

James wheeled around to face Stevie. Stevie stepped backwards. "Don't...you...dare!" James hissed through clenched teeth. Stevie, normally unruffled by anyone, adult or child, swallowed hard and wisely kept his mouth shut.

"James," Bobby said, "I'm sorry. You're quite right and I do apologize. I acted on impulse when I left the train. I had no choice."

"You—" James started to say, but Bobby interrupted.

Bobby grabbed James by the arm.

"James, I connected with someone who I think knows what you and I both feel deep inside; that we are all in imminent danger. I could sense that when he grabbed me. He issued a warning before putting me to sleep. He told me to leave him to his work; that there was great danger if I didn't do what he said."

The others listened with rapt attention and James' anger melted with the growing awareness that they were falling headlong into a deep and troubling mystery.

"I don't know what is going on," Brenda added, "but maybe this will help. Back in the Abbey, I passed the stranger you chased. I got a good look at a tattoo on his forearm: a wolf's head with some strange words written just underneath.

The words read, *Lupus Occisor*."

7

"Wolf slayer!" James whispered. "Now why in the world would a bloke have that tattooed on his arm."

"How do you know that's what it means?" Brenda asked. "It sounds like an ancient language."

"It is," continued James. "And that's what's wrong with the education system in both our countries. You aren't taught the classics anymore, are you? It's Latin, is what it is, and when I was just a lad, Latin was a subject we all loved to hate. It set us straight with language and literature, it did, and if you kids today..."

"Yeah, okay," Stevie interrupted, "so we now have the one occasion where Latin might have come in handy, which, by the way, I could have Googled anyway. The point is..." Stevie wilted under James' glare and slowly drifted into silence.

"The point is," Bobby picked up, "we know what it means, but we really don't know what it means. In other words, who is this stranger? And what is a 'Wolf Slayer?' And what did he imply when he told me to leave him to his work? What work?"

They stood there, dumbfounded, curiosity working at the edge of their thoughts, with an overall look of shared confusion.

"I don't know, Bobby," uttered Stevie. "I think this guy is trouble. He tried to hurt you, no denying that. He even threatened you. As far as I'm concerned, he's up to no good and it's up to us to stop him." Stevie fished out a few stones from his pocket, unaware he was even doing so.

"Maybe," said Brenda. "But then again, he could have hurt Bobby badly, but it sounds like he was trying to warn him instead."

"You say warning, I say threat." Stevie shook his head.

Finally, James spoke.

"We won't know anything at all until we find out who this chap is. Goathland is a very small community so we shouldn't have too much of a task in that regard. Someone is bound to know something. Once we locate him, we'll need to confront him, preferably in a public place. I can be pretty persuasive when I need to be, so I'm not too worried about getting the answers we need. I was a bit of a boxing champion back in the day," he added proudly.

"We're going to have to do this without my mother or Miss Sally knowing anything about it, though."

"That's not a wise course, lad," said James. "Miss Sally lives here and may be of some practical help, while your mum works for the Yard. If she can't help us conduct an investigation, who can?"

"I understand your wish to involve them, James. Especially my mum. She's very smart and has solved some crimes no one else could for Scotland Yard. That's why she's so successful there. But I think she'd never believe what you and I both know; that there is something very dangerous at play here. I could feel that from you when we first met, and I felt it from this stranger when he grabbed me from behind. The fear I noticed in you, I could feel in his touch. It was the same fear. The fear of a reality no one else would believe. Especially someone as rational as my mum." Bobby looked at his mates, who now stared back at him.

"We've had some experience with that kind of thing last year," he continued. "And when we tried to get help from the authorities, nobody believed us. We had to solve that mystery on our own and we're going to have to figure out this one by ourselves, too." Bobby paused a moment, then added, "Before we left the hotel for dinner last night, James, you started to tell me how this all began. Why don't you tell us now?"

James looked at this motley crew in his charge and thought about Bobby's words. He knew Bobby was right. Maybe it was best to get some answers before seeking help from Sally and Melanie. He decided to keep a close eye on these four while they searched for information regarding this stranger.

His decision made, James took a deep breath. "All right, then. It all started about a week ago..."

Constable Reginald Wigglesby, of the Whitby Police Station, stood before his mirror that morning waxing his long thin mustache, ensuring that the edges were properly curled. He plucked at his eyebrows, not allowing them to get too unruly, and finished by brushing his teeth with the same attention to detail. He put on his neatly pressed uniform, donned his cap, went out to his newly purchased Kia Picanto and crawled behind the wheel. He closed his eyes, held onto the steering wheel and breathed deeply. It still emitted that new car smell he loved so much. He turned the ignition and gently pulled away from the curb in front of his flat.

Constable Wigglesby was based in Grosmont, a small village in the northern section of the North York Moors, part of the Esk Valley. Even though he was connected to the Whitby Police Station, his job was to become familiar with some of the smaller villages in the area: places like Egton, Glaisdale, Beck Hole, and Goathland. While the Whitby Station was responsible for policing the moors, this was part of a new policy to bring a more personal touch to monitoring the area. His job was to meet with community leaders and prominent citizens, listen to their issues and be the first official on the scene to address any legal concerns that required police attention. More often than not, he was needed for calming purposes only; reassuring the locals that no matter what their worry, all would indeed be well.

He hated his job. He viewed his assignment as a punishment for informing the Whitby District Chief Superintendent that this whole idea was a wad of rubbish and a waste of taxpayer money. Chief Superintendent Stafford, for some reason, didn't see things that way and promptly assigned Constable Wigglesby to his current task. And, he was told, if he failed at it, his next assignment would be a transfer as a liaison officer to a pensioner hospital in Sussex, where he could spend his days playing gin rummy with the old folks. Wigglesby pondered this as he made his way to Goathland and decided that the best way to handle these yokels was to get them under control with a firm, commanding and professional hand, despite his Superintendent's warning to be warm and friendly.

James repeated the story of the butchered sheep, but this time with more detail. He began slowly, as if he was afraid to tell it. He indicated how a hiker had stumbled across the scene and ran to the Wolf's Head Inn to inform someone of the atrocity. James happened to be there at the time, and, since he knew the area well, he raced off to see if he could do anything. He hadn't believed half of what the hiker had said, thinking that he must be exaggerating. When he got to the site, however, James was confronted with a scene for which he had not been prepared. He knew instantly that the hiker, if anything, hadn't been explicit enough about the carnage. In retelling the story to Bobby and his mates, James spared no details about the gore he found at the massacre.

He told them of the bleated screams that reverberated in his mind and the visions that plagued him as he walked the grounds of the devastation. He spoke of the smell of fresh blood and foul predator breath that assaulted his nostrils at every step. He couldn't visualize what had actually happened, he added, but he did catch flashes of bright moonlight, vicious claws, spurting blood and sharp teeth out of the corner of his eyes. And when he tried to look directly at the images that teased the edge of his sight, they vanished like a puff of smoke in a strong wind. When he finished his story, James wiped the sweat off his brow, pale at his memory of such butchery. No one spoke. The thought of placing their lives on the line once more, as they did last year, was none too appealing to any of them.

"There's more, though, isn't there, James?"

James's head snapped up in question. "Yes, but how did you know?"

"I saw you fidgeting," said Bobby. "You were opening and closing your hands and shifting on your feet. You also kept opening and closing your mouth, as if you had something else to say. Now is not the time to hold back, James. What is it?"

"I'm a strong man," he barely whispered. "And I'm not afraid of anything on this earth. At least I wasn't until this happened. I didn't ever want to have to admit this to anyone, certainly not to Miss Sally and not to any of you, but now I feel I must."

The four of them stood still, listening intently, knowing that they were on the verge of hearing something that needed their full attention.

"As I stood there looking at the aftermath of this terrible scene, I began to shake. It started with my legs and worked up from there. I thought I was tired at first and I looked for a spot to sit down. Then my arms shook badly and that was followed by my head. Soon,

8

Sally finished vacuuming the main lobby of the Wolf's Head Inn in anticipation of the Goathland town meeting that was to be held there today. Her common space was one of the few in town large enough to accommodate such a gathering. She was looking forward to the community getting to see some of her recent renovations. There was more to do in the hotel, most notably in the upstairs guest rooms, but what had already been accomplished in the hotel reception area was quite stunning. She looked around at the handiwork and had to admit it was all to her liking, with perhaps one exception. She wasn't as fond of the sparkling drapes as James had been. Why he had insisted on brocaded fabric with woven threads of silver was beyond her. Sure, they were beautiful in their way, and she did say he could have a hand in redecorating, but they had cost more than she had wished to spend. If it weren't for James' assurance that he would negotiate a deal for them, she might not have gotten them at all. And then, when James finally went to pick them up at the Dandy Drapery Shop, she hadn't realized he'd secured them for every room at the inn. Well, perhaps when renovating some of the upper rooms, she'd think of something else, swap them out, and donate these drapes to charity.

Constable Wigglesby drove through the small hamlet of Goathland with a look of mild disgust. Sheep dung everywhere, he thought. This was clearly not his sort of community. It was too small, had too many farmers and other unsophisticated types, and, well…too much dung! He pulled in front of the Wolf's Head Inn, killed his motor and listened to the blessed stillness that filled the interior of his new vehicle. The inn's outdoor car park was already full, so he decided to leave his car outside the front entry. With a twinge of hope, he entertained the thought that if things got boring, he might be able to pull off a quick escape. He knew, however, that in short order he would soon be listening to a cacophony of common calamities that ranged from minor neighbor disputes to potholes that hadn't been filled to answering such pressing questions as, 'What's being done about cleaning up the public greens so the common folk could use them, eh?' As if the police had anything to do with regulating the potty movements of all of these filthy beasts that pinpricked the countryside. He was made for other, more sophisticated police work, and he viewed this assignment as nothing short of an attack on his breeding and character. Well, he thought, there was naught to be done about it, but take a deep breath, face the music and deal with this local rabble.

As the door closed behind him, Wigglesby removed his hat and placed it under his left arm. He took two large steps into the foyer and looked about in a state of mild surprise. People dotted the interior in small groups, accompanied by a small plate of crudités in one hand and a glass of white wine in the other. They were fashionably, though casually dressed (not a pair of muddy boots among them), and if one listened closely, and he did, there were intelligent conversations going on about world affairs and other pressing business outside the realm of the wee town of Goathland. The Constable gulped hard and moved further into the room.

Stevie's father was a lawyer and he often spoke of the 'dead silence' that filled a courtroom during an especially poignant moment of a trial. When he was much younger, Stevie thought that phrase funny and never quite understood its meaning. He knew it now, though, as it aptly described the mood that followed James' speech. No one spoke a word or moved a muscle. All eyes were on James, who stood with his hands on his knees, breathing heavily. It was Stevie who took the first step. It was a small one, at first. He moved, almost imperceptibly, towards the hunched man. Next, Michael moved forward, followed by Brenda and then Bobby. Within a split second of each other, the four travelers encircled their guide in a group hug of encouragement. James lifted his hands in surprise, not knowing what to do or how to respond, never having had this kind of affection and backing his entire life. At last, he patted their heads, murmuring his appreciation. Bobby stepped back, as did the others.

"We're five now, James," said Bobby. "All for one and all that. No matter what happens in the days ahead, we are all together, here for each other."

"Thank you all," replied James. "I cannot tell you how much I value your support. Even yours." He reluctantly smiled at a grinning Stevie.

"Now what do we do?" Brenda asked.

"A good question," Bobby said.

"I think we go back and get started looking for this guy," Stevie said.

"I want to go see the Whalebone Arch on that hill," Michael surprised everyone with his request as he pointed to the western cliff with one hand and the sky with the other. They all looked at James as if for guidance.

"Well, we don't know where this man is at the moment," said James. "He could still be here, or he could have gone somewhere else. We are supposed to be enjoying ourselves, so to return home now would raise too many questions. We don't want to arouse any suspicion, so our inquiries will have to be carefully planned and executed with extreme caution. I would agree with Michael and say we should explore the western side of Whitby. It will give us time to think, and perhaps develop an intelligent approach on how to determine who our adversary is and what he's up to."

"Like capturing and then torturing him until he spills his guts, right?"

"As I was saying," James continued, irritated at Stevie's interruption, "it's also possible we may see

The old man was down the flight of stairs and nearly out the exit door when Bobby saw him. He was hunched a bit but stood with his right hand on the door handle. He turned as if he knew Bobby was there and looked him straight in the eye. He smiled; a crooked, rueful smile.

"Hello boy," he shouted, almost gleefully. "I told you to leave, didn't I? There's still time, you know, but you'd better hurry!" And with that, the man Bobby had seen in the tunnel underneath the York rail station, the man who had grabbed his leg as he passed him in the tunnel, was gone in an instant.

People were only too happy to oblige Constable Wigglesby, with his insistence on 'moving things along,' so they hurled questions at him that kept the officer on the heels of his feet. Most people in attendance were quite happy with the arrangement that allowed sheep to graze on public land, so that was not an issue at all. Instead, they peppered their guest with a variety of pertinent questions related to big government and taxes, procedures related to the new police policy that governed their jurisdiction, and progress on a number of pending investigations that were now grouped under his umbrella, none of which the Constable had studied before his arrival. Consequently, he stuttered his way through the beginning phase of the meeting, perspiring, pulling on his tie and casting desperate glances for a rescue towards Sally and Niles, who stood only a few feet away.

Bobby was stunned. No doubt about it, he had just been issued another warning. Who was he? What did he want? Once over the shock of seeing him again, Bobby leaped down the steps and pushed open the exit door. He looked back and forth and caught a glance of the beggar as he rounded a corner, heading up towards the Whalebone Arch. Bobby sprinted after him.

As Bobby chased the stranger up the hill, Brenda and Stevie arrived at the exit and sat watch. They stayed put for an impatient ten minutes, watching group after group leave the attraction, but no sign of Bobby.

"It's time," Stevie announced.

"Wait a minute more," said Brenda.

Another group opened the door and they both stood up, hopeful.

"Let's go," said Brenda when Bobby didn't show.

"What about James' direction?" asked Stevie.

"We're wasting time, I think we missed him."

They both raced to the front of the building.

Michael had his eye on the front entrance, but James was pacing. He saw Brenda and Stevie come around the corner shaking their heads. No Bobby.

"What now?" asked Stevie, not too sure of himself for once.

J. M. Kelly

"Can I get you all to stay in one place for a few minutes?" asked James. "I'm going to walk through this place quickly, just to ensure Bobby's not anywhere in there. I'll do it fast and be back here in ten minutes. When I get back, I'll have a plan." They shook their heads in unison and James ran inside.

"Okay," said Stevie, as soon as James was out of sight, "let's bolt out of here."

"Are you crazy?" shouted Brenda. But Stevie, and then Michael, who knew Stevie's sense of humor, smiled mischievously. "I was just kidding."

"Not funny, you moron," replied Brenda. Stevie and Michael couldn't help but let a nervous laugh engulf them, causing bystanders to pause and wonder at their silliness. They laughed so hard, even Brenda couldn't help but smile and shake her head. The boys finally stopped and had just begun a conversation about what to do next, when James came up behind them, walking fast.

"Oi! He wasn't there, I'm afraid. Here's what we're going to do. We'll continue to make our way up to the Arch. Bobby is aware of our original plan, so he'll stick to that and look for us there. It's not that far, so we don't need to rush, and we do want to be careful to look for him on our way. Does that make sense to everyone?" Stevie opened his mouth to speak.

"Good, then let's be off," James finished, without waiting for a reply.

James led the troop up to the Arch. Haggersgate became Pier Road and they passed the famous Magpie Café and the unmistakable smell of fish and chips, rumored to be the best in England. James' stomach

75

growled in hunger, as they passed the quaint restaurant. He was tempted to stop, but didn't dare, not with Bobby still missing.

Continuing upwards, they soon passed the Fun City and Funlands Amusements. It called to Stevie, especially after his demonstration of skills at the summer fair last year. The sound of games being played, barkers shouting encouragement and bells signaling victories at video games, drew Stevie over to the action, like a cat to catnip. He walked, almost in a trance towards the excitement.

"Where does he think he's going?" James asked.

"Don't worry, I'll get him," said Michael, who trotted over to Stevie, picked him up over his shoulder and carried him back to the group.

"Not this time, buddy," said Brenda. "We need to find Bobby."

They turned left onto Khyber Pass and the Whalebone Arch lay ahead. The Arch consisted of two fifteen-foot bones from the head structure of a Bowhead whale. They stood vertically, bending in a bow shaped curve until the narrowed tips converged and crossed at the top, forming a wide arch. They were erected in 2003, replacing an even older and larger set. England had once been a nation with a thriving whaling industry, and this arch was a tribute to the daring and courage of the many sailors who went to sea to ply their trade. The group walked slowly, inexorably towards the center of the arch and stood directly under it. They looked around. Bobby was nowhere in sight.

9

Sally recognized that the Constable was ill-prepared for the barrage of questions being shot at him, and therefore ill-equipped to handle them. She took pity on him and thought she would help by posing what she thought was a fairly easy question, as it related to a well-known incident that had occurred in the not-too-distant past.

"Constable," she began, "not long ago, we had some sheep that were attacked in the hills, fairly close to here. Some have argued that it may have been a wolf and others have suggested a big cat, such as a puma or a panther. Are you aware of the incident and do you have a theory as to what might have attacked them?"

A smug smile crept across the Constable's lips, exposing a small gap between his two front teeth. He finally felt on firmer ground here, having fancied himself somewhat of an expert in the field of British wildlife.

"Preposterous," he said dismissively, ignoring the fact that Sally was doing him a favor by asking him such a question. "Neither theory holds an ounce of water, by my way of thinking. It's positively absurd to think there are either wolves or big cats roaming the English countryside willy-nilly in search of a lamb chop dinner. Wolves are virtually extinct in this country, and big cats are for conspiracy theorists and those believing in Bigfoot and the Loch Ness Monster."

"But what about that Puma found in the eighties?" enquired a senior citizen from the rear of the room.

"Yes, yes, yes, I know the story well, of course, but you do realize that particular cat was an escaped pet, which could apply to any supposed sightings one may read or hear about today. No, ladies and gentlemen, I tell you unequivocally there are no wolves or big cats in these areas, or in the whole of England, and it would be foolish, at best, to indulge in such ludicrous fantasies."

That seemed to put the matter to rest as everyone got immediately quiet, sensing that Constable Reginald Wigglesby was not one to entertain differences of opinion. Wigglesby looked about the quiet room. Seizing the opportunity to close the discussion and escape to his car, he put on his hat, quickly thanked everyone for their kind attention and moved towards the entrance.

But before the Constable was able to reach it, the front door banged open and a sheepherder that lived nearby rushed in drenched from head to toe in blood. He mumbled incoherently and immediately collapsed to the lobby floor.

It was Michael who noticed him first. Not far from the Whalebone Arch was a statue in honor of Captain James Cook, the famous sailor and explorer. The seven-and-a-half-foot bronze statue sat atop a pedestal and partially blocked the group's view from the standing Arch. Encircling both monuments was a lower ramp of metal benches for the aged and the weary, allowing for an excellent view of the harbor and water, far below.

"There he is!" shouted Michael. Everyone looked where Michael was pointing Motionless, Bobby sat on one of the benches gazing out to the North Sea. They rushed towards him. Bobby didn't look up at them, but sat still as a painting, not moving a muscle or saying a word.

"Bobby, are you okay?" Brenda knelt down next to him.

"He came to warn me again." Bobby still didn't look up. "He somehow knew where I'd be and he came here to warn me again."

"Bobby," Brenda gently pushed, "who came to warn you? Who are you talking about?"

Finally Bobby turned his head towards Brenda, who gently put her hand on his knee. The others stood by holding their breath.

"Who, Bobby?"

"I don't know," he whispered.

Sally screamed and the others looked on in horror.

The sheepherder was completely smeared with blood. It soaked his shirt and ran down his arms. It smudged his face and covered his throat. He looked as if he had found a pond of blood and decided to take a leisurely swim. It turns out, that wasn't far from the truth. Melanie took immediate control. She demanded several pillows, one for the man's head and two for his feet.

"He may be in shock, so place those two under his heels." Melanie gave him a quick examination, then pointed at a coat to lay over him and keep him warm. Sally grabbed the Constable's raincoat and draped it over the prone and bloody body resting on her lobby carpet. Wigglesby started to argue the use of his coat, but while leaning over, he got a good look at the massive amount of blood and made a hasty retreat to find a loo, as bile quickly rose to his throat.

"The blood isn't his," Melanie stated to no one in particular. "Whoever it belongs to will be a mystery until he comes around. Bring me some water, please." Someone handed her a glass of water and she patted the stranger's face with it, wiping off some of the blood. The herder coughed awake and tried to sit up.

"Gently," she cautioned.

He regained his wits and looked at the frightened faces around the room.

"I knew there was a meeting today and you'd all be here, that's why I came," he garbled. "It was horrible, it was." He took a sip of the water Melanie held out to him. He choked as he swallowed too much at once, then caught his breath and continued, looking directly at Melanie.

"My sheep, some of them get lost now and then, you know?"

Melanie knew that people under stress needed to talk, to tell you their whole story so they could make sense of it themselves. She also knew she'd get more out of him that way than by interrogating him, since he was still in a state of delirium, so she let him continue at his own frenzied pace.

"And after what happened to those other sheep a while ago, I decided to take my rifle and go find the ones that went missing." A pitiful look overcame him and his voice quivered.

"I drove my four-wheel ATV and went to the area where they were last grazing. It was a few kilometers away. I searched good and wide for them, I did. I didn't see hide nor hair of them anywhere, so I went down a long slope to a glade where I know there's water and shade, thinking they might have taken shelter there overnight. I was going a bit too fast, I suppose, and I didn't see the rock ahead, so when I hit it, my ATV overturned and spilled me out."

His face blanched and he looked positively catatonic. There wasn't a sound to be heard. Everyone stood still as a statue, hanging on his every word.

"I fell right into it," he stammered. His voice rose and tears fell from his reddened eyes. "I landed in a pool of water, or at least that's what I thought it was. At first, I couldn't believe my good fortune to have done so, as it broke my fall and kept me from getting too banged up. But when I was able to sit up, I noticed it wasn't only water. I was doused from top to bottom, covered in thick, red blood. I scrambled up and..." He was shaking. "I...I..."

"It's okay, sir," Melanie said. "You don't have to continue right now if..."

"No, Miss, I have to. I...I screamed and screamed, for how long I don't know. When my legs could finally move, I backed up, but I tripped and fell. I tripped on a root and I fell on...on..." The herder wiped his mouth and peered at a ghastly memory only he could see.

"I fell on a body," he cried out. "At least, my mind told me it was a body, but it wasn't whole! It was in little, chewed up pieces! There were scattered pieces of a torn and tattered dress next to the body parts. I...I knew that dress. I'd seen it before, I did. It was bloody, but I knew I'd seen it before."

At that, he looked up at Sally and stared mournfully.

"It belonged to Penelope Roberts, Miss Sally. Your chef. It was her dress I saw."

✝✝✝✝✝

"All right lad," said James. "Tell us the whole story and leave nothing out."

Bobby did as requested. He told them of his episode at the York rail station: of the smell in the tunnel as he and his mum crossed under the tracks, of the dirty old man who grabbed his leg, of the warning he imparted and how he vanished from the area shortly thereafter. He told them of his tingly feeling as he passed the Dracula Experience and how he was compelled to seek out its source. And lastly, he told them of seeing the old man again at the exit door, his renewed warning and how he chased the beggar up the hill to this spot, only to lose him in the crowd. When he finished, there was silence. Finally, they all closed in to quietly reassure Bobby of how happy they were that they had found him and that he wasn't hurt.

"But you can't do that again," admonished James. "You can't disappear on us and send us off on a wild goose chase in a state of panic, every time you get a feeling or see something not quite right. Agreed? If we're to work on this together, we need to trust and lean on each other for support. And that means sharing what you know or what you think you know, at all times. After all, we're a group of five, not one."

"Okay," Bobby said, embarrassed that he acted so impulsively. "You're right."

The others took a seat next to Bobby on the bench while James leaned against the fence across from them. His back to the North Sea, James leaned forward and spoke softly, to prevent other tourists from hearing him. "We'll need to leave soon and make our way to the train station for the ride back. It's getting near sunset, and I don't want to have to walk too much of a distance in the dark when we return. It may be dangerous tonight."

They nodded in unison.

"Before we go, let's review what we need to do," James continued. "We need to find out who this old bloke is that spoke to you at the York station, Bobby, and then again here at the Dracula Experience. He obviously knows something. We also need to find out about the waiter from the Me and Ewe Pub. We need to find out what his intentions are; after all, he grabbed you here at the Whitby Abbey. I have a strong suspicion that he's at the center of all this, and we're going to have to approach him with a great deal of caution."

"If we need to follow anyone without them knowing

it, I'm your pick," shouted Stevie. "I'm pretty sly about it; they won't even know I'm there."

"Oh yeah?" teased Brenda. "I seem to remember you got yourself in a pretty bad fix last year when you tried that," bringing up that horrible memory when Stevie was kidnapped and left for dead.

"Hey, that was unusual, and you should talk! Look what happened to you!"

"Okay, you two, last year was something we'd all like to forget," said Bobby. Michael, sitting between Brenda and Stevie, just put his arms around them both.

"I don't think we're even going to know what else to do until we find out who these two people are and what their game is," continued Bobby. "I just wish we had a photograph. It would certainly help in tracking them down. I have a feeling it's not going to be easy to locate either one of them."

"I can draw them," said Michael. "I've been practicing since I last saw you and I'm pretty good at it. I draw pirates mostly, but if you tell me what they look like, maybe it will come out right."

"I didn't know you could draw!" said Stevie. "When did that happen?"

"I practice at night. I don't want anyone to see my drawings until I get really good at it."

"That sounds great, Michael" offered Brenda. "When we get back on the train, let's work on that waiter. We all saw him, if even only for a short while and each of us might be able to offer something helpful. Then, maybe later, Bobby, you and Michael can get working on that old man. It's too bad we can't bring in your mom. I'll bet she'd remember what he looks like."

"Yeah, maybe I can ask her what she recalls about him and see if anything comes up. I can tell her that I think I saw someone that looked like him in Whitby. She might not mind talking about it either, especially since she is probably bored out of her mind going to Sally's dull town meeting."

With that they made their way to the Whitby train station, with a quick stop, courtesy of James, at the Magpie Café.

10

The odd-looking structure at Rosedale (fifteen miles from Goathland) was all that was left of an old Cistercian Priory—a home for a particular sect of nuns. It was referred to as 'remains' for so long, no one gave it much thought. The only thing still standing of the former nunnery was a small, rounded old tower. It stood silently at the end of a meandering dirt path, a short hike from the local church, alone and sadly forgotten. Tall and empty, it remained steadfast, a sentry against all that would proclaim itself modern; a throwback to a past that saw wealthy Lords and Barons in control of the land as well as the people that inhabited it. Ignoring such places in modern times was easy. Progress saw the old structures stripped of their basic building blocks, their stones plundered; commandeered to build schools, churches, and other communal edifices. The ancient buildings, the ancient past and the ancient ways were neither appreciated nor acknowledged by those in present times. Until recently.

The Priory was being rebuilt. The lone remaining tower, with a surrounding wall, had been under construction for almost a year. It now resembled a medieval keep, or fortified tower, and served as a home base for a reported recluse who was to live there. Those who were prone to gossip told of a suspicious, middle-aged man of means who had purchased the property; 'A country home,' said one; 'A laboratory,' said another; 'Perhaps the legend of Frankenstein is alive and well, and we'll need to storm the castle at some point,' half-chuckled a third. The truth was, no one had a clue of the stranger's intent. The new owner, who had paid a handsome price for the dilapidated structure, uttered not a word of his desires to anyone. He moved only in the shadows and spoke only in whispers, and rarely interacted with anyone in the larger community. He was an outsider by definition and by choice.

Correspondence with the builder had been conducted through an intermediary, until the tower and wall were completed. The owner was never present while the work was in progress. Where he was during this time was anyone's guess. No one had made his acquaintance, nor caught sight of him in public. It wasn't until the job was done that nearby residents noticed habitable activity in the old tower. They saw flickering lights in the evening, splashing through the shaded windows until all hours of the night. They were the lights of old, however, ones that sputtered with flame, not electricity, casting scant illumination while creating darkened shadows of suspicion throughout the interior. The few, half-hearted efforts at trying to meet the new arrival, made by those citizens motivated by both good will and curiosity, were met with silence or muffled rejections from behind closed doors. After a time, no further attempts were made, and the odd stranger's desire for solitude was reluctantly accepted by the populace. Soon, concerns of who this outsider might be drifted from the collective consciousness of the locals, who, once again, went about their daily tasks.

The owner, unbeknownst to them all, was a direct descendant of an ancient family. He was a man with great wealth; money that was hidden in bank accounts across Europe, allowing him access to enormous funds at all times. It was money that could finance a home built from an old Priory and let him live whatever lifestyle he chose or needed. He would want for nothing and he cared for nothing. He had but one need. One focus. One desire.

To hunt.

✝✝✝✝✝

"Someone fetch the good constable, please," commanded Melanie. She used a dampened washcloth to wipe the face of the herder, who, exhausted from his tale, lay partially unconscious and a touch delirious amidst the turmoil surrounding him. By that time, the local doctor had arrived. He had assisted a child birth that morning, so he had been unable to join the community meeting. Upon hearing of the incident from someone sent to retrieve him, and after the birth of the child in question, of course, he turned care over to a local midwife and dashed over to the Wolf's Head Inn.

"Thank you, Miss, I'll take it from here," he said to Melanie.

"Yes, Doctor," she said. "I'm from Scotland Yard

and have some training in first aid. Is there anything else I can do to help?"

"No, thank you. I'm giving him a tranquilizer and I've phoned for the volunteer ambulance corps. They'll be taking him to the hospital in Whitby and I shall accompany them. When he's ready, I'll notify the police that they'll be allowed to speak with him."

At that moment, a vehicle stopped outside the inn.

"Ah," he said turning his head to the opening door. "Here they are now."

Both he and Melanie moved out of the way so the paramedics could load the sheepherder onto a stretcher, pop him with an IV and carry him to the ambulance for transport. The doctor bid his farewell and joined them.

About that time, Sally's cleaning woman, Mary Childres, who helped out at the inn a few hours each day, had arrived. Sally had called her immediately after Melanie knelt to attend to the herder. She came prepared, armed with an assortment of pungent cleaning fluids, a bundle of clean rags, a fresh mop and a large bucket. She started cleaning the moment she trudged in, moving everyone deeper into the interior of the main room. Melanie allowed her to do so, after saving blood samples from the herder.

A hardware store shopkeeper and a Bed and Breakfast owner accompanied Constable Wigglesby out of the loo and brought him over to the small bar perched in the corner of the large lobby. One of them poured the Constable a glass of Glenlivet, which he gulped instantly.

"Ladies and Gentlemen," recited Melanie. "Please take a seat. Constable Wigglesby and I will be taking statements before you are allowed to leave, I'm afraid."

"Is that really necessary?" asked Sally.

"I'm afraid so," Melanie responded. "It shouldn't take too long and we'll need them for the official record. Just making sure we all heard what we heard and that we can compare the impressions of everyone here. Then, the Constable and I will..."

"Wait just a moment," shouted Constable Wigglesby, grabbing a napkin off the bar and wiping vomit from the front of his splattered and stiffened tunic. "I'll decide what's to be done, here. Apparently, a crime has been committed. This is my jurisdiction and not Scotland Yard's. Therefore, I shall be leading this investigation."

Melanie gawked in surprised amusement.

Now," he continued, "I believe we'll be taking statements from everyone present, so don't anyone dare leave until we have done so."

With his hands on his hips and his feet spread apart, he scanned the room.

"Hello! What's this? Where's my suspect? And where are his bloody clothes?" He licked his lips and marched towards the lobby entrance. "I demand to know who took my suspect?"

"That would be the paramedics, Constable," said Melanie. "The doctor who attended him called the ambulance and left with the patient moments ago. He'll be at the Whitby Hospital for a few days, I'm afraid."

"And who gave the doctor the authority to impede

my active investigation?" he barked.

"I believe he made that judgment based on the health and well-being of the gentleman who collapsed on our floor," Melanie said drily.

"And since you are with the Yard, Miss..."

"Holmes, Melanie Holmes."

"Yes, quite. Miss Holmes, do you mean to say you didn't have sense enough to keep the potential criminal here until I have had a chance to interrogate him? And you there," he shouted at the cleaning lady, not missing a beat. "How dare you disturb my crime scene! Stop what you're doing at once."

"Potential criminal? Crime scene?" responded Melanie.

"Of course," he whined. "The man was encased in blood. Obviously, he was involved in some sort of criminal activity, making him a number one suspect and this...," he waved his hand across the room, "this area is a crime scene. Plain as the nose on your face. And you let him get away before I could break him down and find out what he's been up to."

"First of all, you were a bit...how shall I delicately put it... indisposed to be asking anyone anything, let alone engaged in 'breaking down' anyone. Secondly, the sheepherder is not a criminal suspect. He came here voluntarily to inform us, despite his obvious physical and emotional strain, of a terrible event that he had stumbled upon. Thirdly, and I should think this was obvious, he'd been up to his neck in someone else's blood, samples of which I have saved, so I would hope you will help me sort this out quickly, so we may approach and examine the real crime scene, which our sheepherder bravely described for us before he lost consciousness."

Stymied by her verbal comeback, the Constable cleared his throat, narrowed his eyes, and could only come up with, "Well, we shall see about that."

Melanie swiftly passed a pad and pen around the room. Once people filled out their name, address and contact information, they met with either her or Constable Wigglesby. They were asked a few brief questions, quickly agreed upon by both interrogators, thanked for their cooperation and allowed to leave. When the room cleared, Melanie pulled the Constable aside and spoke quietly. "I'll be in touch with your superiors on the way to the real crime scene to see about officially assisting in this investigation. May I advise you in advance to be cooperative?"

Before he could respond, Melanie turned and spoke to one of the meeting attendees she had previously interviewed. He had related to Melanie that he knew the spot referenced by the herder and he volunteered to take them there.

"Grab your coat, Constable, and...oh, right, you can't do that can you? Well, then, let's proceed, shall we? You drive Constable, and Mr. ah..."

"Jones, ma'am, Samuel Jones, at your service."

"Yes, right then, Mr. Jones, here, will sit in the back and provide directions. Off we go."

Once in the car, Melanie asked Mr. Jones to direct a befuddled Constable Wigglesby, as she made a quick, perfunctory call to the Whitby Police Station and asked to be connected to the Chief Superintendent. She outlined the situation carefully, did not disparage the Constable, and, in fact, made it appear as if he had things organized and under control. She then listened attentively for a minute or two and handed the cell phone over to Wigglesby, who dutifully pulled over to the side of the road before saying hello.

"Sir..." he stammered. "But, Sir... but..." And finally, "Yes Sir, of course, Sir, whatever you say Sir." He continued to look straight ahead, handed her the phone and started up the car.

Melanie listened for a moment more. "Yes, Sir, thank you Sir, I will." She put her phone away.

Wigglesby harrumphed and kept quiet for the remainder of the ride.

"Just ahead is a small dirt road," said Mr. Jones. That'll take us towards the dale. There it is on the left. Turn there, if you please. Now we drive on for about two kilometers and there will be a marked footpath on the right. We pull over there and walk another kilometer to our destination."

"What?" exclaimed Wigglesby, "We walk? A kilometer?"

Melanie was glad she wore flats to the meeting today. "It appears so, Constable, as we do not have an all-terrain vehicle."

"See here Miss Holmes, my Chief Superintendent told me I must work cooperatively with you but I must protest. I have neither an overcoat, thanks to you, nor proper hiking shoes to go traipsing about the countryside." Sensing her anger, he softened his argument by saying, "Perhaps we should notify the Whitby Office for more assistance on this."

Melanie stared at him a moment. "It's a shame

your Chief Superintendent has a limited budget and cannot send out anyone else without a proper assessment first. We need to make that assessment. Nor can he afford to have this become a bigger mess than it is already. So, as you now well know, he's allowed me to work with you on this case in a spirit of professional cooperation. With that in mind, I suggest we proceed to take a look, make some notes, and come to a determination as to what we do next. Agreed?"

Wigglesby paused a beat, then softly said, "Agreed."

Mr. Jones led them down the dirt path, which arced its way around a hillside toward the glen below. They walked briskly, sliding once in a while, losing their footing on an occasional patch of mud. It took them approximately twenty-five minutes of careful, thoughtful walking. The air was cool and the sun low in the sky. No one spoke, each silently preparing for the dreaded scene ahead. When they got close, Melanie turned to Mr. Jones.

"You stay here," she whispered. "Constable Wigglesby and I will proceed to the site. We'll be a few minutes examining the area, then we'll report back here for the hike back to our vehicle."

Jones nodded, and the two officials forged ahead. They rounded a bend, pushed their way through a clump of trees and saw a small opening. They paused at the edge of the clearing. There was a strong smell of copper and the discolored grass was flattened; not smoothly, as if from a roller, but looking more like there had been a struggle, with the flora being crushed and shoved in various directions.

The trees blocked the wind to a soft flutter, so it felt warmer down in the dale, yet they shivered nonetheless. They carefully tiptoed ahead, their eyes sweeping the area for clues of any type. Melanie held out her hand and they stopped. She was keenly alert, barely breathing as she scanned the site. Wigglesby had the look of a frightened owl, his head swiveling from side to side and his eyes bulging.

"Just ahead, see that tall tree along the edge?" Melanie exhaled. Wigglesby's wide eyes focused on the red slashes, crisscrossing the base of the large oak. Next to it, lay a pool of crimson water, a horde of black flies buzzing about, landing and taking off like the planes at Heathrow Airport on a busy day. Strewn across the earth were clumps of what looked like raw meat, and there, hanging on a moving bramble bush, pushed by the gentle wind, swayed a piece of the shredded dress described by the bloodied sheepherder.

"Constable," said Melanie. When he didn't respond, she looked in his direction. Wigglesby was as white as a sheet and dry-heaving.

"Constable!" she said again, louder his time. "I need you to focus. I need you to examine this scene as dispassionately as possible." Wigglesby stared at her, as if from a distance.

"Reginald!" She used his Christian name. That got his attention. "Can you do that?" she said more softly.

He swallowed, although his mouth was dry, and nodded. Then, they both walked closer to the horrific tableau, simultaneously removed a writing pad and pen from their pockets and started taking notes.

11

Actually, James had nearly thrown a temper tantrum unless they stopped for some fish and chips at the Magpie Café, drawn as he was by his growing hunger pangs and the smell of his favorite dish. Since they all found themselves hungry and had enough time remaining, no one was disappointed with the decision. Although Stevie preferred a cheeseburger, he wilted under James' stare and had the fish.

After dinner and en route to the train, they stopped at an office supplies shop and purchased two sharpened pencils along with a ream of drawing paper. Bobby and the others kept a sharp lookout for the waiter from the Me and Ewe Pub, but no one caught even a glimpse of him.

"Where do you think he went," posed Brenda, as they settled into their train compartment a bit early.

"I think he's in disguise," said Bobby, drawing everyone's attention. "Think about it. He confronted me, so he knows that I know something about him. Which means, he must also fear that we're actively looking for him. We need to prey on that fear. We need to do a search."

"I agree," said James. "But we have to be very cautious."

97

"We should travel in pairs, at least," said Stevie.

"Why that's the most sensible thing you've said to date," responded James.

"Thank you, my good ma..." Stevie wisely decided not to finish his statement.

Michael, his finger pointing upwards, stated the obvious.

"I think we should get a sketch first. I can do it pretty fast."

No one disagreed, so they leaned over the back of Michael's seat to watch him work. Beginning with Bobby's recollection and encouragement, Michael drew an oval shaped head on the blank sheet, refining it, as Bobby made suggestions.

"I learned this from watching a television show that taught me how to draw," said Michael. "The artist said that all faces are oval, so that's where I should begin. My mom taped the show for me; I watched it over and over again." Bobby remembered how watching movies repeatedly made Michael an expert concerning pirates, which had aided them so much the previous year. He hoped it was the same with his skill at drawing.

Michael erased the rounded cheek area, bringing the lines in closer to create a more angular face. Several attempts resulted in crumpled sheets of paper until he got it just right. It frustrated him when he made mistakes and he would rather begin again than work with too many errors on one sheet. Michael's frequent stops and starts made his mates anxious, but they were used to Michael by now and let him continue in his own methodical fashion.

J. M. Kelly

Melanie noticed that the road had darkened
quickly. There were no streetlights on the moors.
Fortunately, the moon was once again full,
illuminating their path. Wigglesby, Melanie and Mr.
Jones were on their way back to the inn, traversing the
dirt road that would take them to the main road and
then on to their final destination. No one said anything
since they'd left, but their fear was palpable. The car's
high beams shot like lasers into outer space, grabbing
their mute attention, as if in a trance. Out of the
darkness on the left side of the road, a large, black,
shadow-like creature darted across the road in front of
them.

Wigglesby hit the brakes with enough force to send
his passengers forward, jolting against the rigid seat
belt that, fortunately for them, held them in place. The
car stopped sideways, it's rear facing the direction of
the shadowed figure they nearly hit.

"Bloody hell!" shouted Wigglesby.

"Did you see that?" screeched Mr. Jones.

"I did," whispered Melanie.

Melanie reached for her purse and retrieved the
Smith and Wesson Model 10 revolver she often carried.
In her role as Special Investigator, she was one of a
minority in the British police that frequently carried
a firearm, both on and off duty. She clicked off the
safety and slowly stepped from the car.

Stevie was about to enter car number four when someone grabbed him from behind. He was wrestled into the loo. The door was slammed shut and locked. Fueled by fear he started kicking, fighting his attacker with every bit of energy he could muster. Out of nowhere, the stranger produced a roll of duct tape, wrapped Stevie's arms and mouth, then his legs. When he was properly trussed up, he was secured to the toilet with even more tape. He got a good look at his nemesis, who wore no disguise or makeup. He looked exactly as Michael had drawn him. He leaned into Stevie's face, breathing heavily.

"You have a lot of spunk for a slight fellow. I know you all are trying to find me. Don't. That course shall bring you nothing but pain and sorrow. Perhaps even death. You must leave me alone."

He unlocked and opened the door a crack, peeked out, then turned to Stevie once more.

"Your friends will find you easily enough. You've forced me to take my leave early and I'm not happy about it, as I have much ground to cover tonight. But for the last time, I warn you, leave me be or you will die."

He let himself out and closed the door. He reached over to the emergency brake lever and pulled. The train came to a grinding halt, but while it was still moving at a rapid clip, the stranger leaped, rolling down an incline into the tree-covered hillside. When he slowed enough to stand, he ran as fast as he could through the brush.

Anyone standing on the train fell forward, grabbing onto the seats or compartment doors for lighter shade of dark. The full moon in its waning phase provided the real light at this time of the evening. They left the station as a tight group and walked the short distance to the Wolf's Head Inn. They looked like a brood of chicks, scurrying around James, their mother hen.

"Did you hear that?" blurted Stevie. They were halfway home.

"No," Bobby said confidently, but Brenda whispered, "Yes, I think I did."

Everyone was quiet, their eyes boring through the thick shrubbery that surrounded them. Just ahead on their left, some of the bushes shook. Everyone focused on that area. Dry twigs cracked and the wind blew an unpleasant odor in their direction. Stevie fidgeted with the stones in his pocket. Michael had his finger pointed in the air and slowly smiled.

"What the heck are you laughing at, Michael?" asked Stevie.

By this time, James shook his head, calling himself foolish, while Bobby and Brenda joined in on the laughter.

"What?" urged Stevie.

Michael just pointed towards the shuffling in the bush ahead. A large, shaggy ewe poked its head out and bleated at them all. Their nervous laughter chased the fluffy sheep back into her nesting area for the night.

Melanie and her group pulled up to the inn just as

James and the youngsters arrived. Mr. Jones had stopped shaking five minutes before they got there and barely had enough strength to get behind the wheel of his own vehicle to drive home. The Constable appeared wan and Melanie had a look of abject fear.

"Mum, what's wrong?"

"Inside," was all she said, as if the night was listening.

They entered the inn and proceeded to the kitchen, where Sally was making tea. James locked the front door behind them, all the while saying they were now safe and secure. Everyone looked at Melanie, including the Constable, who subconsciously deferred to her in this time of sudden fear and crisis.

"Constable Wigglesby here, Mr. Jones, a local man, and I were at a crime scene today. Without getting too graphic, I will tell you that we found the remains of Sally's chef."

Brenda gasped, Sally clutched her arms tightly, and James placed his face in his hands.

"The scene was bad. Enough to make me say that I do not want any of you wandering around the countryside, especially at night. But that's not all. We saw something on the way back here. It ran in front of our car."

"It?" asked Bobby?

"The Constable and I didn't get a full view of it, only a rough gauge as to its size and power, but Mr. Jones did. He insisted on leaving for his home as soon as we got back here," she said absently, "and we had no cause to keep him. But before he left, he told us what he saw..." She paused, staring into space, then started again. "I've never seen a man so afraid."

"Mum," Bobby whispered. "What is it? What did Mr. Jones see?"

"He said, he saw a monster on the moors."

12

T hose words gave their imagined fears shape and substance. Took their scary thoughts and made them real. 'Monster,' she had said, giving the horror a name.

Melanie spared them the details of the crime scene. She told them of her encounter with the dark shape along the dirt road. Her voice shook, describing how the car skidded...how she took her gun and approached the hidden beast...how it roared in anger when she neared...and how it attacked their vehicle as they raced for their lives.

"It would seem," said James, "that we are going to have to organize a search party in the morning, eh Constable?"

Wigglesby cleared his throat and tried to regain some of his bravado. "Right. I...uh...you know the locals you can trust," he said turning to James. "Get together a handful, no more than six men, who are adept with both guns and tracking. Bring them here in the morning and we'll all go out to the spot where we saw this...er...thing, and we'll see if we can turn up anything useful."

He looked up at Melanie for approval and she gave

him a silent, imperceptible nod. "I'm returning to my apartment tonight and I'll be back here at eight sharp. Good night." He then turned and asked James to accompany him to his car. "Just so you can lock up behind me," he added, but the truth was he didn't want to go out to his car alone.

When James returned, they had discussed going to bed and everyone moved toward the stairs. Melanie stopped Bobby. "Bobby and I need to talk, so we'll stay up a little longer." Stevie stopped and stared at Bobby, but Brenda grabbed his arm. "That does not include you," she said, and pulled him out of the kitchen.

"I'm making myself a cup of tea, Bobby, would you like one?" Melanie said when they were alone.

"Yes, please."

Melanie boiled the water and prepared their tea. It was clear she was organizing her thoughts.

The tea steeped and felt warm as Bobby wrapped his hands around the cup. It smelled like home. Melanie looked at her son.

"I need you to be straight with me, Bobby. I've enough experience as an investigator to know that you haven't been."

Bobby stared at his mum and tried to look innocent, but knew he wasn't fooling her.

"Mum, I..."

"Please don't lie to me, son. I'd rather you said nothing than lie."

"I won't, I promise. But I can't tell you everything. Mostly because there's so little that I know. I know that you are aware of my gift...this ability to see images that are supposed to help me think clearly.

Lately, it's had the opposite effect. If anything, what I see confuses me."

"Maybe if you share your thoughts with me, I can help sort it out."

"There is something strange happening here. I know you didn't believe me when we arrived, but there was a man giving me a warning in the tunnel at the train station. He wasn't begging like you said. He told me to stay away from this place or I'd die. And then when we got here to Goathland, I had a very strange feeling about things."

"Such as?"

"I don't know, it's hard to say. But, I do feel that there is a great deal of evil here. And I think that the killer of Sally's chef is tied in to it."

There was a long pause.

"Is that it?"

"Yes, mum," Bobby said with his head down. He wanted so badly to tell her everything: about the waiter with the tattoo, the man in the train tunnel who appeared again in Whitby, and most importantly, his visions. But it was the vision of his mum's face amid the bloody carnage in his dream the night they arrived that prevented him from sharing it all. He was determined to keep his mum out of harm's way if he could.

"Thank you for telling me what you could. I know it isn't all of it, but I do need you to promise me something. I need you to not take foolish risks that would put you or your mates in danger, and I also you need to tell me if you find out something important."

Bobby looked up. "I promise."

"Let's go to bed, then."

As he climbed up the stairway, Bobby felt badly. He knew that by trying to protect his mum, he would be breaking his promise and tell her as little as possible. He hoped she would understand. Later. When it was all over.

Not much sleeping took place that night, and everyone left their bedroom doors wide open. People lay in bed staring at the ceiling, listening for any wayward sounds, windows locked and curtains drawn. The alarm in Melanie's room went off at six in the morning. She roused Bobby, who went to shake his mates. Everyone was to gather for a light breakfast in the kitchen at seven.

It was clear when they staggered into the kitchen that no one had slept well. Brenda was yawning, Michael followed suit and Stevie was rubbing his eyes. Bobby shook his head, as if to clear the cobwebs, and Sally, still in her robe and slippers, slowly moved around the kitchen and made tea for the group. There was a plate of pastries on the table, but no one seemed hungry. All were filled with the uneasy anticipation of what lay ahead.

James had been up for hours and was the only one filled with energy. He moved with a specific purpose, having just arrived with a handful of neighbors who now sat in the lobby, each carrying a loaded rifle.

"Right then," he said. "The only one missing is our intrepid Constable." He reached for a pastry and ate with gusto. That seemed to break the spell for the young ones and they dove into the food, hungry at last.

By the time everyone was finished eating and

getting dressed, and the neighbors were on their second cup of tea, the clocks in the lobby chimed eight. On the eighth chime, the front door opened and in walked Constable Wigglesby.

"You there," he pointed at the small grouping of volunteers that he, himself, had requested. "You are no longer needed. You may go home." They looked stunned and cast a questioning glance to James, who looked just as surprised as they.

"Go on, then. I'll be releasing a public statement to your town officials later this morning, and I'm sure you'll be chattering about it in your pubs tonight, but for now, all you need to know is that I no longer need your service. Good bye."

One by one they picked up their weapons and left the inn, muttering amongst themselves. "Follow me," Wigglesby commanded, and led the now stunned James into the kitchen where the others were talking.

"Now see here—" James began. Wigglesby held up his hand for silence and addressed the group.

"I have news and you all will be some of the first to know. We have our killer," he said with a smug smile. There was an audible gasp from Sally, but Melanie narrowed her eyes and listened closely for the rest of the story. Bobby looked at his mates, then back at the Constable.

"It was a black panther," he said. "And it seems I'll have to eat my previous words about no such animals being loose on the moors."

"You said, 'was', Constable?" asked Bobby.

"Yes, I did. It was shot very early this morning by a farmer, out near the area we investigated yesterday.

It was ravaging one of his sheep. The farmer had taken to bringing a rifle with him when checking on his flock, due to the rumors that have been circulating about some beast on the moors, and he caught it red-handed, so to speak," he sniffed. Michael pointed at the ceiling, drawing the Constable's attention to the light fixture. Michael pressed on with his question. "Mr. Constable, sir, where did it come from?"

Wigglesby frowned at Michael for daring to interrupt him, but answered, anyway. "It was an illegal pet, obviously mistreated and made vicious by its owners' abuse. It was being transported from Scotland to the Yorkshire Wildlife Park. Apparently, the ignorant possessors of this illegal pet had heard of the good work with animals being done at the park and, having tired of owning it, planned to drop the beast off at the entrance by chaining it to a gate; after hours, of course. They drove it down to Middlebrough by lorry, and then proceeded along roadway 19 southward. Near the intersection of roadway 170, they had a flat tire, spun out and overturned, thereby, releasing the unfortunate animal into the wild. It immediately raced across the moors, half starved, creating a killing path in its wake. It was spotted near Helmsley and then near Hutton-Le-Hole, putting it on a direct path to Goathland and the surrounding area. And to that I say, case closed!"

"Why didn't we know about any of this?" asked James.

"I only heard about it very early this morning from the Whitby office. Apparently, the idiot owners of the panther were afraid of what might have happened and didn't report it at first. It was only after a thorough investigation of their lorry crash that it was brought to light. Also, no one took these sightings very seriously, as they have happened from time to time in the past with no real results. It usually involved a witness who'd had a few too many pints. And, none of this was put together in the Whitby office until the beast was shot and killed earlier today."

"What do you mean, 'obviously'?" asked Melanie.

The Constable looked confused.

"You said, 'It was an illegal pet, obviously mistreated and made vicious by its owners' abuse.' I'm asking, why is it obvious? Did the owners confess to mistreating the animal? Did it show signs of physical abuse? Do we know for certain that it killed Penelope Roberts?"

"Of course, they didn't confess to mistreating the animal. They're stupid, but they're not dumb. Just follow the facts: It was caught eating a sheep, we know of at least one other sheep that's been killed by it and you don't have to be Agatha Christie to figure out who killed Ms. Roberts, when this beast was caught in the exact same area."

Melanie opened her mouth to respond, when he added, "This case is closed, as I've already indicated."

"We'll know more when the forensics team from my York Office investigates the crime scene," said Melanie.

"I've canceled that request, actually. I've also dispatched a crew from Whitby this morning to clean up the area and remove all traces of what happened, so no one else stumbles upon it."

At the look of shock and surprise on Melanie's face, he added, "With my District Chief Superintendent's approval," and smiled.

"I am on my way to the scene now to oversee the cleanup," he went on. "The facts, as they stand, will confirm my analysis beyond a shadow of a doubt, and we can now all move on from this dreadful business. Er, at the request of DCS Stafford, you are welcome to join me at the site," he reluctantly said to Melanie. "But you may not get in the way or obstruct my team in any way. Is that clear?"

She nodded, but said, "I will make some calls along the way, of that you can be sure." She then turned to Sally. "Sally, do you mind..."

"No, no, we will all be fine, you go ahead, I'll see you later. Not quite the vacation you had hoped for is it, but there you are."

After they left, Sally began cleaning up and said, "Well, such a horrible way for poor Penelope to die, but at least they've found the creature that did it and it won't harm anyone else."

Bobby looked at his friends and whispered, "Upstairs, my room."

Bobby and his mates drifted off to his room. James winked and said he'd be up shortly. They barely arrived when they heard James clomping up the stairs. A moment later, James entered the room and gently closed the door behind him.

"I don't believe that story at all," Bobby said.

"Why not," said Stevie, "it sounds like it could be true."

"Two reasons. For one, I don't feel it, not even a

little. From the time we arrived, I've been emotionally confronted with a series of odd circumstances: the peculiar man in the train tunnel, the stranger at the Me and Ewe Pub, the encounter with him at the Whitby Abbey, the reappearance of the tunnel man at the Dracula Experience, and something that crawled up the side of this building one night while I tried to sleep."

"Wha..." James started.

"You were not aware of that last one, I know, but I do believe that it's all related somehow. I'm more certain than ever that the man with the wolf tattoo is a key to solving this mystery and we need to find him as soon as possible."

"You said two reasons," said Brenda. "What's the second?"

"My mum doesn't believe it either, not for a second. Did you see the way she looked at the Constable? How she questioned his judgment? She believes the murder of Ms. Roberts and the escape of the black panther have nothing to do with each other. And if she has her doubts, that's good enough for me."

"What do we do now?" asked Stevie.

"What we said we'd do," answered Bobby. "We each have a task, and we need to get on with it. I'm heading for the local library and Michael will begin online researching, specifically that tattoo and any history related to it. Stevie, you and Brenda should walk about town as we discussed. Get a map, act like tourists, ask questions and take notes. James, you planned to talk to people at the Pub. Let's meet back here for dinner and we'll compare notes."

They all nodded, ready to do their part to solve the mystery.

"Just be careful," Bobby added. "I think the evil we face is far more dangerous and far more ancient than an abused pet panther that escaped."

13

Bobby made his way to the town library. Since the town itself was small, the library consisted of a tiny upstairs room in an old, dilapidated building that had been recently painted a drab gray. The downstairs of the building, which fronted the main street, was a small tourist shop, its window crammed with the work of local artisans and mass-produced trinkets alike, each indistinguishable as they fought for the attention of vacationers. Bobby never gave them a second look, as he pushed open the door, located to the right of the picture window. It allowed him access to an old, indoor staircase with a banister that would take him to the library upstairs.

Bobby paused at the bottom step and looked upward. There was another door at the upper landing; a large, solid looking, polished wood door. It shone in the hazy light cast upon the stairwell from the one, dim light bulb that hung just above the landing. Bobby took a tentative step upwards. A loud, painful creak groaned from the belly of the large first stair. He paused, keenly aware of the noise he made. The next stair sounded worse than the first. Each succeeding step brought renewed sounds of misery to the enclosed area. By the time he reached the top, he thought the entire village must have heard his ascent.

The heavy door had a cardboard sign that read OPEN, dangling by a cord from a nail poked into its facade. Bobby leaned towards the door and listened. He heard nothing inside. He reached for the handle, a large, round one, made of polished silver. He clutched the handle, turned it clockwise, pushed it open and stood there a moment, his mouth agape. He let go of the door, which closed automatically behind him and stepped inside.

What he saw was not what he expected, as it contradicted the eeriness of the entry. The room was brightly lit with the warm glow of soft bulbs, not the harsh, overly bright, tubular incandescent lighting you often find in public places. Although small, the room made good use of the space available. Tables that would seat four people were carefully arranged throughout, their chairs neatly tucked underneath. A small row of five new desktop computers flanked the outside wall, each perched on a desk with a cardboard corral providing a modicum of privacy. To the left of the tables, stretching from the front of the room to the rear, were five rows of stacking shelves, each with an impressive collection of novels and reference materials for such a small community. And just inside the door to his right, sat a small, elfish man with a broad, infectious smile, perched at a neatly organized desk. He slowly closed the opened magazine that was spread before him and turned to Bobby.

"Hello there, young fellow, welcome to the library," he said brightly in a slight Irish brogue.

"Hello."

"How might I help you today?" he asked.

Bobby looked at the tiny man. He was short and round with a thick tuft of reddish hair sweeping backwards along both sides of his balding head. His bifocals were perched atop his tiny nose and the way he grinned gave him the appearance of an amused leprechaun. His small feet barely touched the ground and he swung them forward and backward, as if keeping time to a silent tune only he could hear. No one else was in the library, presently.

"I'm here visiting a friend of my mum. She owns the Wolf's Head Inn, where we're staying."

"Oh, you mean Sally Jenkins! Yes, yes, she's quite a wonderful person, a patron of the library. Dedicated to the improvement of our fair community and the education of our youth, and all that. I'm proud to say that I know her well." He extended a hand in greeting. Bobby took it.

"My name is Patrick O'Reilly," he continued. "I'm the librarian. I'm originally from Ireland," he said, again with a slight Irish lilt. "I came across this wonderful village on my way to Whitby, many years ago in my youth. They needed a librarian, I needed a job, and the rest, as they say, is history." He laughed, a full belly laugh, which brought a smile to Bobby as well.

He clasped his hands and rested them on his expansive mid-section, tilted his head to the side and asked with a smile, "Again, young man, how can I help you."

Bobby hadn't had much time to plan how he was going to approach his quest, especially with this man asking him questions.

"I'm here to explore and look around," Bobby answered vaguely, as he briefly cast a glance around the room.

"Is that so?" The librarian's eyes seemed to pierce Bobby's soul. "Please do have a look, then. If you need anything, anything at all, please call out. I'm happy to help you." He picked up the magazine in front of him, and seemed to resume his reading, although he was clearly watching Bobby over the rims of his glasses.

Bobby walked toward the shelves, feigning interest in several books, some of which he picked up to examine. He made his way to the back of the room, moving in and out of the aisles created by the tall racks. He paused when he reached the Animal section, then again in the Local History sector. When he crossed the room and took tentative steps to the computers, Mr. O'Reilly piped up.

"Laddy, why don't you tell me what has you so worked up and how I might direct your search?"

Bobby snapped his head up. "What do you..."

"Come now, boy, I could tell you were looking for something specific, as soon as you came in. And the way you paused at the Animal and Local History areas narrowed that down a bit, although you clearly didn't find what you are looking for. You continued and still could not locate a part of our library that may be of use to you."

He paused a moment.

"So, young man, for the fifth time, how may I help you?"

Bobby decided that he was going to get nowhere

fast, unless he faced the risks of securing assistance. But he was doubly wary of enlisting the aid of adults. His experiences the previous summer proved to be a disaster in that regard. He hesitated a moment longer, and then decided he was going to have to tell this man what he was searching for, or, Bobby was sure, he would not find it on his own.

"I... uh... I'm looking for information on a phrase that I saw recently. It's an old phrase, and I'm not quite sure where to look."

"Well what was it boy, spit it out, then!"

"*Lupus Occisor.*"

The librarian blanched at hearing that ancient phrase spoken aloud. Beads of sweat formed on the ridge of his brow. He stood slowly, Bobby noticed, with a slight tremor in his hands.

"Where did you hear that?"

His dry voice barely rose above a whisper. He took a few tentative steps towards Bobby. Bobby instinctively backed up a step.

"I'm sorry lad, I don't mean to scare you, but I need to know where you've seen that phrase and whether or not there was an accompanying picture."

"I saw it on a man's arm not too long ago. It was a tattoo. And yes, there was a wolf's head alongside of it."

The librarian almost staggered backwards. A handkerchief suddenly appeared. He wiped his forehead and exhaled loudly. Then he slowly walked to the entry door, opened it, turned the card around so it read CLOSED, and let the door whoosh shut.

Then reached over and locked it.

Brenda and Stevie walked the main street of Goathland, stopping every so often to look around and take in their surroundings.

"How the heck are we going to find out anything interesting around here," Stevie moaned. "There's nothing really going on in this dull town and it's not exactly a big place. We'll cover it in no time. And then what?"

"I don't know, Stevie. I'm not sure what Bobby had in mind sending us out here, or what we're supposed to find out. This town is small, I agree with you there. Just keep yourself open for anything. Something will happen. Always does. Has to."

They both looked up and saw an elderly man sitting on a park bench in the middle of the town square. Sheep roamed the area, munching on the grass lawn. The old man seemed oblivious. He wore a tartan tam, a thick, beige fisherman's knit sweater, a rumpled, flannel shirt and brown corduroys. He chewed on the end of his black, battered Meerschaum pipe, and viewed the two youngsters from under the brim of his cap with clear, sharp blue eyes. Stevie caught the village elder staring at them and returned the look. Neither blinked. Brenda also noticed the attention he paid them. Intrigued, she grabbed Stevie's arm and moved him towards the wooden bench.

"Whoa, what's that smell?" gasped Stevie as they got closer.

The old man chuckled, lifted his feet, banged them together and shook off a large clump of lamb dung.

Stevie started to head back to the main street, but
Brenda grabbed his arm and stopped him. She sat on
the bench and turned to the stranger.

"I'll bet you see a great deal go by here," she said.

"Aye," he said with a Scottish accent, moving his
unlit pipe from one side of his mouth to the other.

"I'll take that as a yes," mumbled Stevie. Brenda
shot him a look that shut him up.

"Have you noticed many strangers around?" she
continued.

"Aye. Lookin' at two right now."

"We're looking for a particular stranger. If I
described him to you, do you think you could tell me if
you've seen him recently?"

The old man stared at her a moment.

"Mebbe."

Stevie blew out a deep breath and rolled his eyes.

A cloud paused in the sky, blocking out the sun.
The wind kicked up a notch, the air grew cooler and a
shadow passed over the area.

"Brenda!" Stevie whispered. "Let's get outta here.
This guy is creepy and we're wasting our time."

But Brenda ignored him and directed her attention
at the elderly gentleman next to her.

"Have you lived here long?"

"Aye, all me life."

"As I said, I'm looking for a particular stranger,"
she said. "Someone who has probably come to the
community recently."

"Whit fer?"

Stevie grabbed Brenda's arm and pulled. "Come on
Bren, lets go. Chatty Kathy here is going to tell us

absolutely zip."

Neither Brenda nor the old man paid any attention to Stevie's whining.

"I don't have much to tell you," she said. "Mostly because I don't know much myself. But I do know that this stranger is the key to a mystery. He may be the problem, or he may be involved somehow in the solution. We'll know more if we get a chance to speak to him. But for that, we need to find him first. He's tall, he has dark hair that's combed down the middle, an intense stare and a funny tattoo on his right forearm. I think he works at the restaurant."

The elderly local man looked over at Stevie and stared, making Stevie uncomfortable. He chewed his unlit pipe, moving it from one side of his mouth to the other. He then looked at Brenda again. He paused, then leaned towards her and spoke. His breath had the sweet smell of a strong cherry flavored tobacco that cut through the aroma of lamb manure, as it gently tickled her nose.

"Seek out the Travelers, lass, they'll tell ye what ye need to know, as they know all of the strange happenings about." He then tapped his pipe on the arm of the bench and stood on shaky legs. He tipped his hat and walked away.

"Wait," she cried. "What...."

But she didn't get to finish. The old man kept walking as he shouted, "The Travelers, lass! They'll tell ye!" He waved his hand in a small goodbye gesture as he disappeared down an intersecting path.

14

"Please sit down," Mr. O'Reilly said to Bobby. He pulled out his handkerchief again and once more swiped his forehead. He looked nervous and afraid, not threatening at all. He absently pulled out a chair that was tucked under one of the tables and plopped into it.

Bobby sat on the opposite side. He leaned forward so he wouldn't miss a word.

"I was afraid of that," said O'Reilly, softly. "How much do you know?" he asked, as if he were weighing how much he was going to tell Bobby.

"I know enough to know that we are all in danger, and that the person I'm looking for is in the middle of the mystery."

O'Reilly waited. It was obvious that he was wrestling with the idea of sharing his information. Time stood still for what seemed like an eternity. Then, it appeared as if a decision was made, and he was ready to unburden himself of something important.

"Well then, I have a story to tell you, my boy, one that will force you to suspend belief. I urge you to listen without question until I finish."

Bobby nodded and the librarian took a deep breath.

"It all began with King Edward I," he began, "who reigned from 1272 to around 1307. The countryside was different then. There were fewer cities, of course, and certainly far less people. Wildlife was abundant and that allowed for an explosion of wolves throughout the country. They began destroying crops and eating domesticated sheep. Complaints from hamlets and villages eventually reached the King. He ordered a loyal servant, one Peter Corbet, to rid the land of the irritating and invasive beasts. Peter set about his work with vigor. He and his helpers were accumulating a vast number of wolf pelts. The King paid handsomely for each one collected, and they knew they'd be wealthy when they returned.

Corbet's men began to notice that the attacks on livestock spiked at the onset of a full moon, and those attacks were much more gruesome. Even a small number of farmhands went missing without a trace.

During the next full moon, something happened that drastically affected their plans. Some of Peter's comrades failed to return from a hunt. Peter immediately sent out a search party, but they disappeared as well. A second search party met with the same fate as the first, and Corbet was now down to a handful of five loyal and stout men. Peter Corbet himself led that final group on a mission to find out what happened to their friends."

O'Reilly paused a moment, staring into space, recollecting the tale he struggled to tell.

"They followed an easy trail to a remote part of the moors. They paused on a hillcrest and looked down into a shadowy glade. Near the bottom of the hill, they could see the dark opening of several large caves. Corbet realized it would be a difficult climb down to the entrance of the caves, especially since daylight was fading. He instructed his men to backtrack to the previous hillside and make camp. They would return in the early morning to explore the caves.

That night, in the light of a full moon, they kept their flame low and slept close together, with their backs to the campfire. They hugged their swords and axes, resting fitfully. In the wee hours of the night, a lone man from the second rescue team staggered into their camp, rousing them all to action. He fell at their feet, bleeding from open chew marks on his body. He shook violently as he told them how his entire group had been captured by a pack of huge, manlike wolves.

'Some were immediately slaughtered and eaten,' he said. 'Others, like him, were hung by their feet and turned,' he mumbled, as his voice trailed off. They had no idea what he meant by 'turned' and asked him to elaborate. The poor man gasped desperately for air, collapsed and stopped breathing. Moonlight bathed his body in a soft, eerie shroud and he looked quite peaceful. Suddenly, his back arched, he nearly levitated off the ground and he let out a loud, frightening howl. His body stiffened, he fell to earth and his eyes bulged. Corbet and his men stood frozen, watching in horror as their friend, right before their very eyes, slowly turned into a man-sized version of the beasts they hunted and skinned.

The poor, tortured soul rose from the ground as his facial features grossly distorted into a long snout and his body grew thick, dark hair. His arms and legs tore through his clothes, leaving them in tatters. He stood on bent hind legs putting his full weight on his now deformed toes. He unfurled long, sharp, claws from front legs that used to be his arms, and he stared at his former mates with unconcealed malevolence. He snarled and bared pointed fangs. He stood nearly two and half meters tall and let out a vicious howl that could be heard clear across the valley."

Bobby, in rapt attention, shivered from fright, as the diminutive chronicler told his tale.

"He looked at each man in turn, breathing a low growl, readying for an attack. But Corbet and his men wasted no time, despite their chilling fear. They drew their weapons instinctively. Two men pretended to attack from each side diverting the creature's attention, while one of the men from the rear drew his huge silver sword across the back of the beast. It screamed in pain as Peter, who stood in front, swung his axe down, nearly splitting the animal in two. The beast fell with a thud. They all stood in terrified silence, unable to move or take a breath.

Then they heard them.

Horrific howls. From every direction—from the front, the sides and more from the rear of their camp. Peter and his men formed a loose circle, keeping their backs to the fire. They readied for battle. In an instant, the surrounding beasts pounced. It was a bloody melee; a mixture of arms, claws, teeth, swords, bits of flesh and flying gore all at once.

Those brave men fought with singular determination. Their only thought was to defeat their enemy. When the battle was over, only two men were left standing, both covered in blood from head to toe. Seven wolves out of the ten that attacked were on the ground dead. Three had escaped and could be heard howling in the distance. Corbet ordered that they cut off the beasts' heads and burn the bodies, including those of their comrades. When that task was accomplished, Corbet's last remaining friend fell to the ground. He looked up at his leader with sad eyes and told him he was bitten.

Corbet pledged a sacred oath before his dying friend that he and all of his descendants would continue to hunt these beasts until they were fully exterminated from the earth, no matter how many generations it took. He then turned melancholy eyes towards his friend, raised his axe and ended the man's life."

Brenda and Stevie looked at the back of the old man until he disappeared from view. They then stared at each other with a puzzled look. "Did we hear that correctly?" asked Brenda.

"What the...?"

"Easy Stevie!"

"No Brenda, I'm sorry, but this was a complete waste of time. That geezer was playing with us. What he said didn't help at all, and he did nothing but jerk us around."

"I don't think so, Stevie. True, he wasn't clear about what he shared, but we do know something we didn't before. He said 'Travelers,' right? Did he mean tourists? People on vacation? Anybody that happened to be a stranger in the village? Let's see if we can find out what he meant by that."

"How are we supposed to do that?" asked Stevie in exasperation.

"By making it one of the questions we ask other people. Let's move on and see what else we can find out. If we talk to anyone else today, we'll ask them about these mysterious 'Travelers' he mentioned."

Stevie shook his head, not optimistic at all about their chances of finding out anything helpful, but they plodded on together, moving along Main Street and pausing at the shops along the way. They didn't have to go far when a small group of three British boys their age fell out of a candy store entrance, known as the Sweet Shoppe, a tangle of arms and legs, laughing and pushing each other, collectively bumping into Stevie.

"Whoa, watch it!" Stevie exclaimed.

"Sorry mate," said a tall blonde haired young man, who appeared to be the leader of the group. "Meant no harm." He spoke to Stevie, but he was clearly looking at Brenda with interest. Stevie noticed and wasn't too pleased about it. Each boy had a paper sack in hand, filled with a collection of fragrant sweets. Instinctively, the leader extended his bag towards Brenda and Stevie.

"Care for some? My name's Bryan."

"No thanks," Stevie grunted with a scowl.

"I will," Brenda answered with a pleasant smile and reached into his bag. She pulled out a couple of tasty looking candies that resembled the gummy bears she used to get back home.

J. M. Kelly

"They're Jelly Babies," said Bryan. "And these are my mates, Roland, the short stubby guy with the red cheeks, and William, the quiet one here. Neither one speaks much. They're not slow or anything, I just do most of the talking. Right guys?"

Roland and William nodded in unison.

"Hmph," uttered Stevie.

"Hi," said Brenda pleasantly, chewing on a Jelly Baby. "I'm Brenda, and this is my friend, Stevie."

"Are you Yanks?" asked Roland.

"No, we're Russian spies," answered Stevie.

Brenda wanted to find out what these boys knew of the stranger they were looking for and so she invited them to sit along a low wall next to the shop. Plus, she didn't mind spending time with Bryan. Stevie was not amused.

Bryan offered her more sweets, but she declined.

"We all live here in the area, although a bit spread apart," said Bryan. "Our folks work at the RAF base over in Pickering, which is how we all got to know each other. Each summer, we visit one another and spend time at each other's houses. William lives closer to Goathland, so that's where we are this week." William nodded his head.

"How about you two?" asked Bryan.

Stevie still seemed disinterested, although he kept a watchful eye on Bryan. Brenda spoke for the both of them.

"We're from America visiting a friend of ours. He's on vacation here in the North York Moors and we're all staying with a friend of his mom's at the Wolf's Head Inn."

"Oh, Mrs. Jenkins," said Bryan. "William's mum and Mrs. Jenkins know each other quite well." William kept nodding. "Perhaps while we're all here in Goathland, we can do something together?"

"Nope," said Stevie, and, "That would be great!" said Brenda, both at the same time.

Bryan flashed a crooked smile at Brenda and said, "Brilliant, I'll ask William's mum to call Mrs. Jenkins to arrange it. Cheers!" The boys then took the short walk back to William's house.

"Well, that was nice," said Brenda.

"Yeah, just great, but you forgot to ask them anything about the stranger we're looking for, or the Travelers that old guy mentioned." Brenda blushed at her obvious forgetfulness. "Well, we'll see them again, soon, I'm sure," she said, trying to recover from her error. "Come on, let's continue." She then moved toward the store, just vacated by the boys.

✛✛✛✛✛

"What happened to Peter Corbet?" asked Bobby.

"Legend has it that he returned to the King with whatever pelts they had, and reported on what he had witnessed. To prove he did not kill his mates for the riches he would receive for the pelts collected, Peter asked that the wealth be divided among the heirs of his dead mates. For himself, he asked only for his share which would be used to rid the land of this new pestilence that came in force with the full moon. He vowed that he alone and all of his descendants forever, would seek out and destroy these beasts until the earth was rid of them."

"How do you know all of this?" asked Bobby.

The librarian gave Bobby a half smile and closed his eyes for a moment as if he needed to concentrate on an important decision. When he opened them again, he looked straight at Bobby, rose, tilted his head towards the back of the library, and said, "Follow me, lad."

Bobby pushed back his chair and followed the Irishman. They approached a door that was hardly noticeable, along the back wall between two cluttered shelves. It was painted the same color as the surrounding wall, with no window or obvious handle. The librarian reached into his pocket, pulled out a remote control device, pressed it once and the door popped open. He glanced at Bobby before pushing it all the way and entered.

Bobby followed him in, both wary and curious, but ultimately trusting his intuition.

The room was dark, lit only with a low watt lamp, perched at the edge of an old wooden desk. The desk was made of polished solid oak, its strength hidden under a pile of loose papers, opened books and a variety of loose manuscripts. The air was musty and there was the faint hum of a dehumidifier playing alongside a central air conditioner keeping the room both dry and comfortable.

"The pages in this room are delicate, you see," said the librarian. "The temperature and humidity must be maintained so as to not ruin what I've been examining."

"What are you examining?" asked Bobby.

There was a brief pause. The librarian stared at

Bobby before replying. "The personal diary of Peter Corbet."

"But where did you get it? And what about this room?"

"That's a bit of a story, as well."

Ringlets of wispy smoke crawled out of the loosely stacked, flat-rock chimney, darkening the already gray sky above the small, clapboard shack that nestled in a small clearing. It rested there for a moment, a curled, threatening presence of foreboding evil. A sudden gust of wind swept by, picking it up and sending it helter-skelter. Muffled sounds could be heard within the dwelling, a singsong incantation that was not unpleasant to the casual ear. The truth was much darker, however, as the words became clearer to a more cautious listener.

"There is a beast that roams the eve,
And guided by the moon,
His rage is great, when the light is full
To meet him is your doom.

You cannot hide, there is no dark
That frees you of his bite,
Each day he turns, the wolf he takes
And hunts for flesh each night."

Loud cackles followed this dirge, as the three old, bent women who inhabited the cottage went about their business. Blackened moss and dampened twigs were dumped on the low fire, causing additional smoke to spew from the chimney. Something dead and foul was plucked from a glass jar and laid carefully atop the smoldering heap. Its pungent odor crept around the room, seeping into its walls and wrapping the sparse furniture in a cloak of olfactory decay.

The smell didn't bother the three hags that tended the fire. They were, in fact, in a state of rapture, reciting their mantra with tender care, inhaling the tainted air voraciously.

"Oh yes, my dears, it's almost ready," howled one, the leader of the small group. The other two cackled again in a fit of laughter, nearly falling over in their revelry.

The leader's name was Bertha, a direct descendent of Old Nanny, the most famous Westerdale witch of the days of old. She stood at only four and a half feet tall, slightly bent at the waist, her crooked nose pointing towards the wood floor below. She wore a ragged brown jumper, tied about her rounded stomach with a smudged piece of torn rope. A blue paisley bandana was tied around her greasy, gray-streaked hair, accentuating the toothless grimace that graced her face. The other two, named Helga and Hestra, also shared a respected lineage. Westerdale was known, long ago, for its strong witchcraft bloodline. They were of the same height and stature, even wearing similar clothing, distinguishable only by the use of their different colored bandanas: Helga wore red, and Hestra, a pale yellow.

"Is it ready?" asked Hestra impatiently.

"Not yet," said Bertha. "We have to let it sit for a time. He killed that woman for us so that we may live longer, but we mustn't be hasty. He is all alone now, and he cannot kill enough to keep all of us alive forever. He needs to rebuild his den. He needs to add to his pack, with young ones that will help him nurture us. We must be patient. He rests for now, but soon he will be hungry again. Soon, he will hunt and turn them. Then there will be more to feed us and we will be much stronger." Their laughter continued long into the afternoon, their anticipation growing with the thought of expanding their den of wolves.

As far back as the time of the Vikings, stories were told of monstrous dogs in the area of Westerdale. Sightings were frequent of these strange animals that roamed the moors in search of unsuspecting voyagers. Beasts, it was said, that would grind your bones to dust. And if they didn't get you, the witches that lived in the hinterland most certainly would.

"Wander too far," the stories went, "and you'll wander the earth no more! At least not in human form!"

Legends about such creatures were plentiful throughout the ages. They were big, shadowy beasts. They sported long fangs and knotted sinew, and they roamed freely across the moors attacking wayfarers. But, when man became more numerous across the land, those legends abated, quieted by the slow approach of advancing civilization. In time, many believed such creatures never existed at all, that they were a figment of fevered imaginations; tales to tell young ones, ensuring they would be home in bed by dark with the covers drawn tightly to their chins. Fairy tales were written about such beasts over the years and placed in storybooks, helping to solidify their status as nothing but entertaining folklore.

There were those that did believe, however. Some, nay many, held such stories as gospel truth deep within their hearts. And because they believed, they cautiously watched over flock and family, ceaselessly scanning any and all shadows, ever fearful that the beast of their nightmares lurked within, ready to pounce at a moment's notice. The fevered stories they shared among themselves grew over time and with the sheer number of tales came exaggerated firsthand accounts of the shape, size, and ferocity of their foes. In those accounts, dog became wolf and four-legged ground runners became beasts that walked on hind legs, raising their taut bodies to new, more frightening heights. Attacks by the beasts were no longer designed to kill prey, but to torture and destroy their quarry beyond recognition—or so the stories went. No one ever knew for sure, because, as they all knew, if you bore witness to the existence of such creatures, you would not live to tell about it.

Those who believed such things largely kept to themselves. They remained quiet, careful about making their beliefs public, fearful of being called fools, or worse, by their contemporaries. And they learned, over time, that it was never safe to venture beyond their bolted doors and burning fires at night, especially when the moon was full.

Modern man, it seems, has a much shorter memory. He has forgotten not only the ancient

143

legends, but also whatever kernel of truth had spawned them. Stories of old have become fables and falsehoods. If you treated the stories as fact, people would laugh at you, and rightfully so, in this age of logic and reason. Alternative explanations for a slaughtered sheep or a lost herder were always offered by those who thought they knew better; sanitized facts were always much easier to believe than stories of murderous monsters roaming the land. No one nurtured the good sense to heed the ancient warnings any more. And since no one believed them any longer, no one had cause to fear them.

So, it is, in this modern environment of careless neglect, that an ancient beast is free to take shape and roam across the darkened landscape. The creature feeds often in this era of unawareness, but all too often, that is not enough. He isn't meant to merely feed; he is meant to kill. He is a hunter and it needs, as his ancestors did, to instill terror in his prey, to see them wide-eyed and frozen, unable to utter a sound, out of gut-wrenching fear; no sound, at least, until he tears them apart bit by bit.

The beast that still roams this countryside is the last of his line, the sole, remaining member of the Ancient Wolves. He sleeps during daylight and hunts at dusk. Unlike some legends, which say the beast comes only with the full moon, he runs as a wolf nightly, hunting and killing at the direction of the hags that control him, mostly eating stray sheep and small animals. It is only with the cycle of the full moon that he is able to break the chains of the spell that binds him. When that happens, he can—and does—kill indiscriminately. When the moon is at its apex, he can turn a human into one of his own, should he so desire. He almost did so recently with the female he stalked, but reveled in the chase too much, and, in the end, he tore her apart and consumed most of her. It was sloppy of him, but he didn't care.

His kind had always kept their numbers small, even back to the beginning of time. They had an innate fear of being discovered, tracked and eliminated, so they moved about their world with cunning and stealth, honing their hunting skills as time moved slowly forward. Whenever confronted by a pack of humans, they would slaughter them all and feast on their bones. No trace would ever be left behind for others to find. And when their numbers would dwindle, they would ensure their survival by turning a few of their human captives. They merely had to bite them when the lunar orb was full, and, instead of eating them, let them lay for a day as prisoner. By the next night, their victims would turn and become one with the wolf horde. The new members of their group would join the old ones and race across the hills, hunting, feeding and terrorizing, as was their destiny.

But too many had died too fast. Fate had taken a hand and drove them under the control of the haggard witches. After their group was decimated by Peter Corbet, the remaining three stragglers had found their way to Westerdale in the dark. They were hungry, tired, and without leadership. Hence, they were careless. They had approached the small, candle-lit, crumbling shack, perched against a small hillside in Westerdale with little caution, thinking they could easily overpower any human that resided within. Their tongues lolled, dripping with saliva in anticipation of a long-sought, overdue meal. When they had reached the cabin, they knew instinctively that something was wrong, but failed to act accordingly. Food had been neatly placed on the porch, waiting for them. There was a huge hunk of raw meat, dripping with bright red blood that ran in rivulets down the two steps to the ground. Bowls of water lay nearby, calling to their parched throats. Their innate fear made them approach slowly, but their drive for safety was no match for the enticing scent of the blood and cool, shimmering water. They had taken the few brief steps up to the food swiftly, casting their eyes across the area for possible danger and seeing none. Without hesitation, they swooped, tearing the meat apart, gnawing on the bones for the marrow and gulping the precious water. They didn't realize that the water contained a powerful potion, one that had been concocted by the woman peering with glee from the filmy window of the house. By using that potion, that old witch was able to control their pack from that day forward, at least until the span of a full moon. At that time, their bonds were temporarily broken, and they ran free and wild, under no one's control but their own, forced to return under the witches control when the full moon waned.

They had thrived for many years like this, hunting, killing, and turning humans at will, bending to another's will only when compelled to do so. Surviving modern times, however, had been a challenge all its own. In today's world, some members of their pack were killed by accidents on human roadways (the remains removed by others in their group before human discovery), and some died by eating poison. So many were lost so swiftly, that soon, only one remained.

It was clear that this sole survivor had to rebuild the wolf pack. He needed young ones to do this, so they could carry on into the future. He knew where to find them, having once climbed up the outside wall of their dwelling, but he was burned and turned away by a strange substance near the opened window, which weakened him. Once he regained his strength, he would hunt them down and turn them, of that he was sure. He'd also kill and eat the adults that watched them, then start his own pack with the new, stronger, younger ones, and maybe, somehow, rid himself of the control of those hated witches. Soon, he thought with glee and determination. Soon.

16

Michael had stopped working long ago. He had been holed up in his room lost in the research Bobby had requested. Being alone for him was not a problem, it never had been, but as the day wore on, he found himself missing his friends and wishing they were back from their investigations. They had been gone for the better part of the day, and Michael found himself worried about them. While he still had difficulty showing his emotions outwardly, Michael enjoyed a strong bond with his friends, and he was deeply concerned about their safety.

Finger pointing towards the ceiling, he mumbled to himself: "I wonder if anybody found out anything useful?"

"Eh, whassat?" said James, who happened to be passing Michael's room. The door was wide open as James was on his way to do some chores. "Who are you speaking with, boy?"

Michael still had his finger towards the ceiling and continued pacing the room, even though James had asked him a question. He responded by ignoring James, who merely shook his head and continued his journey to the attic.

Michael knew something; something important. He needed to tell someone about it and that someone was Bobby. It bothered him that Bobby was not there. As he looked outside, shadows crawled across the side of the house, and the sun slowly dropped to the horizon. Darkened imprints of tree limbs reached for the upper windows. Evening was coming, and with it, darkness.

What if they are in trouble? he thought. What if they need me? What if I am the only one left to help them?

Michael made up his mind. He was going to look for Bobby. *Where did he say he was going? Right, to the library!*

Without another moment's hesitation, Michael turned on his heels and walked swiftly out of his room, down the stairs and straight out through the front door. He hadn't bothered to tell James or anyone else of his departure. He simply needed to go find Bobby, so he went. It was an error in judgment for which he would later be very sorry.

Bobby stared at the librarian for what seemed like an eternity.

"Go on," he simply said. "I'd like to hear that story."

"Well, as you've probably guessed, I'm not your regular librarian in a regular small country village."

Bobby nodded.

"This secret room proves that more than anything, I suppose. It so happens that I am working for Her

Majesty's government. I am an agent from the Office of Antiquities Phenomena based in London, with a secret office at Whitehall, the very nerve center of our government. I'm afraid it's all very hush hush, and I'm compelled to ask you to keep it so by not telling anyone about my real task here. The only reason I'm telling you, young man, is because I believe you are on the trail of something very dark and evil here in the moors. I've been investigating varied aspects of a story, and trying to piece them together to get a complete picture. And here you come, trotting into my library, seeking information on the very thing I'm studying. I believe fate has taken a hand by bringing you here. I can't help but feel you are a key link between the elements of this story, and I need to find out how."

Bobby was dumbfounded. This small, happy, pleasant country librarian was a spy.

"Are you like James Bond?" Bobby asked.

The librarian laughed heartily. "No, no, no, nothing so dramatic, although I do look sporty in a tuxedo. No, my boy, my job is to find and investigate artifacts, antiquities and strange occurrences throughout Great Britain, but especially here in the North York Moors," he said, warming to his subject. "It's kind of like that television show in America. The X-Files I believe it is called. I've investigated such items as the Rosetta Stone, now housed in the British Museum. It is said to contain the key to understanding hieroglyphs, but there are some who believe it's really a message from another culture from elsewhere in the Universe."

"You mean, like Aliens?"

"Quite so, yes!"

"I've also examined Stonehenge," he continued. "It's quite an amazing marvel, if I do say so myself. I mean really, can anyone deny its basic implausibility? And yet we conveniently overlook that tantalizing fact and provide oversimplified explanations of its origin that the public is willing to accept."

"Like what?"

"Like it was created by an ancient society of men. Rubbish. They couldn't possibly. And I cannot even begin to elaborate about what is contained in the locked rooms in the basement of the British Museum, nor what I've found concerning the reign of Egypt's Amenhotep. You'd be astonished."

"But, what about this room?" asked Bobby. "And that?" he asked, pointing at the diary of Peter Corbet.

"The North York Moors are the most interesting and enigmatic part of England. There is a great deal of mystery here, in other words. There is much yet that needs to be discovered and studied. It's an eerie land with an eerie history. Peter Corbet is an historical fact; he existed. His role in eliminating the country of wolves is also a fact. What is not known by the general public, and at present studied only by me, is the story I previously related concerning a band of Super Wolves."

"Do you really believe that to be true?" asked Bobby.

"That diary is your proof," he said, pointing at the book. "And yes, I do believe it. And what's more, so do you. I can see it in your eyes. There have been clues about the existence of such creatures for years, but they were quickly covered up by bungling investigators and people that were too anxious for a simple explanation. I've been working silently and carefully, trying to amass a body of knowledge that will help us all to better understand the mysteries of our world and, more importantly, keep us all safe. Unfortunately, I don't feel safe. I'm afraid I haven't for a while, now, and I think we are all in a great deal of danger."

Bobby knew that what the librarian said was true and that fate had, indeed, brought him here. He also felt that the information he just heard was leading him and his friends toward a violent destiny, so he had to ask: "Why are you so anxious to tell me all of this?"

Mr. O'Reilly looked up at Bobby and said, "Budgetary constraints play a role, my dear boy. My government is thinking of withdrawing all funding to my department. I need to find proof of this creature's existence soon or they will shut me down. And I believe that you can help me."

Brenda and Stevie were agog at the interior of the Sweet Shoppe. Even though it was a relatively small place, there was candy on every shelf and in every cabinet. Stevie imagined that it smelled like the inside of the Wonka factory. There was, in fact, an entire, glass-enclosed set of shelves devoted to a variety of different flavored Wonka Bars: Chilly Chocolate Cream, Nutty Crunch Surprise, Triple Dazzle Caramel and Whipple Scrumptious Fudgemellow Delight. Their names alone were enticing.

A gentle, elderly woman approached them. She had short white hair, neatly brushed back, and held in place with a collection of clips and pins. She was conservatively dressed in a long-sleeved navy blue dress with white polka dots and navy blue shoes with a slight heel. Her light blue eyes crinkled at the corners, indicating a lifetime of happiness at helping children by plying them with candy.

Before she arrived, Stevie whispered, "Ask her quickly and let's go!"

"Hello, dears, may I help you?" asked the old woman.

"Yes, Ma'am," said Brenda. "Um, can you tell me what your specialty candies are here in England?" Brenda decided to engage the woman in conversation first, an approach that drove Stevie crazy.

"Well," she said, "our most favorite is our Jelly Babies. They seem to go quite fast among locals and tourists alike. But we do have quite a variety. Here, for example, are our Flakes, a melt-in-your-mouth chocolate, our Licorice Allsorts, made of licorice, sugar, coconut, and gelatin..."

Stevie shook his head and walked towards the exit, as the woman went on in some detail about Black Jacks and Fruit Salads, Pear Drops, Maltesers, Double Deckers, and Crunchies. He threw open the door and left, as she mentioned something called Aero Bars.

Ten minutes were pushing into fifteen when Brenda finally emerged, carrying a small brown sack. She walked back to the bench where she and Stevie had spoken to the elderly gentleman not too long ago.

Stevie followed. She sat and extended the bag toward Stevie. "Malteser?" she asked.

"What the heck is...?"

"It's like a malted milk ball that we get back home. They're good, try one."

Despite himself, Stevie took one, popped it into his mouth and angrily asked, "Well, is that it?"

"Nope." Brenda chewed the rest of the candy in her mouth before elaborating. "She hasn't seen the stranger I mentioned, but not too surprising, I guess, since he's probably not the type to go into a candy store." She swiped her teeth with her tongue and swallowed what candy was left.

"She does know about Travelers, though."

"Then spill it, Brenda, for gosh sakes, I'm waiting out here thinking this was a total bust, and, surprise, you manage to find something out, so let's hear it."

"Hmmm, maybe it's because of the way I ask for information, Stevie, instead of barging into a place like an Avengers superhero..."

"Okay, okay, you win, so tell me already."

"They're gypsies," she said.

"Gypsies?"

"Yes, and she told me where to find them."

17

The tension that filled Constable Wigglesby's small car was as thick as a London fog. To make matters worse, he had managed to get a flat tire and had to change it himself, a task he was utterly incapable of performing. The prolonged effort at trying to do so took most of the morning, thereby delaying their arrival at the crime scene by hours. Melanie was so angry she couldn't speak. She had tried but failed to reach her superiors, due to poor cell phone service, adding to her already high level of frustration. The Constable was both smug (for bringing this matter to a rapid and satisfactory—as far as he was concerned—close) and nervous about being verbally attacked by Melanie, who sat icily beside him in the car. She had made it very plain that she did not approve of his assessment of things, nor in his haste to clean up the mess. He decided to attempt a conversation in the hopes of avoiding any issues later.

"So, I suppose you don't approve of..."

"No, I do not, Constable."

"See here, Inspector, you must believe that I have the well-being of the entire community as my utmost interest, and I will not tolerate..."

"You won't tolerate?"

"No, I will not tolerate your interference, nor the

interference of Scotland Yard in this matter. This is my jurisdiction and I not only have complete authority here, I have the backing and support of District Chief Superintendent Stafford in Whitby. Of that, you can be assured. And with his full knowledge, I have concluded that the renegade panther that had been shot and killed this morning was indeed the culprit guilty of wreaking havoc among the locals and the cause of recent mayhem in this area."

"Is that what you call the death of Penelope Roberts? Mayhem?"

"I will not be bullied into saying something that you can misinterpret. You know what I meant. The panther has been killed and as far as I am concerned, this case is closed."

Melanie slowly turned her head in his direction. "That was no panther we saw last night, Constable, and you know it."

Constable Wigglesby remembered how afraid he was last night when that vicious sounding dark shadow slammed into the side of his car. He remembered how that local gentleman, Mr. Jones, referred to it as a 'monster.' He hadn't said it at the time, but when he stepped on the gas and peeled away from the scene, he had looked over his shoulder and caught a glimpse of what stared in the face of Mr. Jones, and that's exactly how he would have described it.

"And perhaps you are wrong, Inspector. It was very dark and our fears were at a heightened level. Then something large and dark threw itself into the side of my car. That is all I know. It very well could have been, and most likely was, the panther in question."

"Don't lie to me, Constable. I turned my head as you did. You saw something much more fearful than a large cat, as did I. We both had a quick look at what Mr. Jones faced. I've been to the zoo, Wigglesby, and that was no panther."

The Constable licked his lips, wiped his brow and fidgeted in his seat. He reached up and adjusted the rearview mirror only because he couldn't keep his hands still. But he would not change his story.

"I saw nothing to alter the facts as they stand. To wit, a beast has been terrorizing the countryside, lately, and early this morning, a wild animal in the form of a runaway black panther was caught killing a farmer's sheep and was shot and killed in response. I see no reason to prolong an investigation into something so plain and obvious in its conclusion. And at the risk of sounding redundant, Inspector, this case is closed."

Melanie sat with her mouth open, staring at him as he drove. He worked his jaw muscles, but clearly was not going to discuss it further. She sat back, folded her arms and stared out the window. There was nothing more to be gained by arguing, Melanie reasoned, so she decided to wait it out until they reached the scene.

Upon arrival, they pulled into a roped off parking zone, which had been hastily constructed far too close to the murder site. A large crew of full and part time bobbies were milling about, improperly attired for a crime scene investigation, some in uniform, some not, but no one wearing crime scene jumpers or booties.

The site was clearly compromised. It was obvious that their task was simply to clean and eradicate, not to investigate. Melanie's heart sank.

Constable Wigglesby hopped out of the car as if he were attending a party, smiling and waving to the bobbies who were going about their business. Melanie slowly emerged from the car, trying to remember where to begin.

"Who's in charge of the cleanup," Wigglesby asked.

"I suppose I am sir," said a bobby in full uniform. "DCS Stafford from Whitby phoned me early this morning and gave me orders to sweep the area clean, dispose of the remains in a respectful manner and write up a full report for his inspection."

"Quite. I'm Constable Reginald Wigglesby, in charge of this investigation."

"Oh yes, sir, the DCS told me to expect you."

"Where are they?" Melanie asked.

"And who might you be, Miss," asked the bobby, in a challenging tone.

Melanie already had her ID card drawn and presented it to the officer. The bobby in charge looked at Wigglesby who shrugged slightly and rolled his eyes. He then tipped his hat and gave Melanie her card back.

"Where are what, Miss?" he asked.

"The remains, officer," she replied lightly, looking about the scrubbed area.

"They were placed in plastic bags..."

"Excuse me?" she interrupted.

"Begging your pardon, Miss, but there weren't enough...um...connected pieces to place anywhere else.

Anyway, they were placed in bags and sent to a funeral home in Whitby for cremation. It was our understanding she had no relatives to contact, and were instructed by DCS Stafford that this would be the best option for a proper burial."

"In other words, there is nothing left to examine, is that right?" she said.

The bobby shifted on his feet, not used to being challenged.

"And we surveyed the area for any evidence before you arrived," he continued, turning towards Wigglesby, who smiled and nodded approval. "My men kicked up the entire grounds turning over rocks and debris, and sifted through the dirt to uncover anything suspicious," he said proudly.

"In other words, they've completely destroyed any chance of anyone with a talent for crime scene investigation to uncover anything at all other than 'sifted dirt!'"

"Now see here, Miss, you've got no cause to question my work. I've followed direct orders from DCS Stafford himself, and I suggest that if you have any problems with them, you take that up with him." He then tipped his hat again and walked away.

Standing there, hands clasped behind his back, Wigglesby looked at her and shook his head. "I'm going to inspect their work," he finally said, and followed the officer.

Melanie trudged over to the area where the actual massacre took place and looked around. It had been pretty thoroughly cleaned up—no remains were to be seen and the area was all but swept with a broom. It would be next to impossible for her to find anything of substance, but she looked anyway. She felt she owed it to her friend Sally to find out what she could about the death of her chef, Penelope.

There were no surgical booties to put on, but she did produce surgical gloves, an evidence bag and a pair of tweezers, something she always packed wherever she went; she was glad she had grabbed them before she and Wigglesby left the inn. She overturned clumps of grass and carefully poked around the tree where the event appeared to have occurred. Most of the area, unfortunately, had been picked clean. She was about to turn away when she noticed something wedged in behind a piece of tree bark. She used her tweezers to extract a clump of dark hair and carefully placed it in her evidence bag. She zipped it up and thought about her find. She was receiving sidelong glances from those still kicking around the area.

"Constable Wigglesby," she shouted.

Wigglesby, who had been chatting it up with the lead bobby, looked bothered at being disturbed. He did, however, walk over to Melanie.

"What is it?"

"That site where we were attacked by the beast, last night..."

"Yes?"

"We need to go there. Now. Before it gets dark."

"Now see here, I am not..."

Melanie leaned in close.

"I'm not asking you, I'm telling you. And if you refuse, I'll have your pension for obstructing an investigation. I'm sure my superiors would take a very dim view of your refusal to help me, especially since I've found something useful to investigate."

Now unsure of himself, Wigglesby began to waffle. He looked around to make sure no one had heard her issue the threat, nodded, and made his way to the car. On the way, he shouted to the lead bobby.

"Carry on, I'll tell DCS Stafford what a good job you've done."

It didn't take long to find the area where the beast had attacked them on the previous night. Both of them remembered it vividly. The car pulled to a slow stop, each inhabitant now reluctant to leave the safety of the idling vehicle. They held a collective breath until Melanie abruptly reached for the door handle and opened her door. It made Wigglesby jump.

"What're you doing?" he whispered.

"I'm getting out of the car to look for something."

She placed one foot out the opened door, drew her revolver and carefully scanned the area. She slowly stepped out and moved in the direction where she had first seen something suspicious.

"I'll sit here and keep the car running, then, shall I?" Wigglesby called after her. Without turning, Melanie waved a hand and continued. With her head down, she examined the ground, moving her head from side to side, all the while listening for any strange noises out of both caution and fear. She paused, narrowing her vision and called out.

"Constable! Come here!"

Wigglesby got out of the car, nervously looking in all directions. He left his door open and the car running. He made his way over to where she stood and, even though he tried to prevent it, his voice squeaked when he said, "What is it?"

Melanie pointed to the ground in front of her. "Does that look like the paw of a panther?" she asked, finger extended to a huge paw print with massive talons. Wigglesby stared, his pale face unable to mask his growing fear. He licked his lips and his voice quivered. "It could be," he said, although he didn't sound like he really believed it.

"I want a cast made of that," Melanie said. "Now."

Wigglesby was caught in a fit of confusion. He wasn't used to making critical decisions like this. He was used to following them only.

"I'll...um...I'll have to call my superiors and...um...I'll let you know."

"Oh, Wigglesby, be a help for once. This is evidence and I need a cast of it before it disappears. Now, your DCS has literally destroyed just about anything of use at the prime site, so don't let that happen here. Have someone come up from the site and take care of this immediately. Then, I promise, I'll get out of your way. I'll take the cast to our lab in York and will get back to you with the results, personally, as soon as it is identified. Please."

Wigglesby thought for a moment more, then nodded an affirmative. He went back to the car where he picked up his cell phone, called the lead bobby, and gave him directions to where they were. It took only a few minutes of driving time. The bobby brought the requested material, which he had in his van, and followed the instructions now provided by Wigglesby. He poured and made a cast with special dental impression material. It was fast drying and when it was done, he picked it up and handed it to Wigglesby, with widened eyes, but no comment. Wigglesby, in turn, handed it to Melanie who placed it in the backseat of the car.

"Thank you, officer," she said. "Now, Constable, please take me back to Sally's. I'll need to retrieve my car and head for York immediately."

"Return to your duties," Wigglesby said to the officer and got into his car.

They moved swiftly, in the direction of the Wolf's Head Inn, kicking up dust under the watchful and frightened eye of the lead bobby.

18

Michael was deep in thought as he headed towards the village. His mind raced, wondering if his friends were in trouble like last year. What a horrible experience that had been. Not only were they pursued by the spirit of a long dead pirate, Brenda and Stevie were both kidnapped and almost died at the hands of that creep. Michael had to admit he was really excited when he and Bobby came to Stevie's rescue, but he could not forget how bad Brenda looked when they finally managed to get to her, and how frightened he was of the pirate when they finally met face to face. He shuddered at the memory.

He kept on in this way for some time, looking at the ground, kicking the occasional stone down the path and thinking about the information he had discovered on his computer—the possible existence of witches in the area. He wasn't absolutely sure if it was important, but he was pretty sure. And whenever he was pretty sure about something, he knew he needed to share it with his friends.

The sun dropped like a stone, and with it, the temperature. Where previously he was hot, even sweating a bit from walking so hard, Michael was now shivering slightly. He had forgotten to bring a coat with him, so he rubbed his arms as he walked, to stay warm.

"So, what are gypsies anyway?" said Stevie.

"Not 'what', Stevie, who."

"Okay, who are the gypsies?"

"I had to do a report on them last year in school and I remember some of it," said Brenda. "They're a group of people that live in many countries, including our own. They first came from northern India a long time ago. I seem to remember that they left because barbarians invaded their country. They spread out in lots of other countries and adopted many of the customs of those areas, but they kept a lot of their own traditions. They move around and never stay in one spot too long. Many of them travel in colorful round wagons. Some of the wagons are pulled by horses still, but lots of them are large vans or campers. They tend not to trust authority because they're badly persecuted no matter where they go."

"Hey, I'd give you an A-Plus for that."

"Well, that's not all of it, but it's all that I remember."

"What do we do now?"

"We go back to the inn and join the others. Michael may have found something, and I'll bet Bobby has."

It was quite dark when Brenda and Stevie crossed the threshold of the Wolf's Head Inn. A full day of exploration accompanied by the stress of seeking information without sounding like an alarmist, took its toll. Stevie was hungry.

"What's for dinner?" he blurted out. James was coming down the stairs and Sally broke through the swinging doors, coming from the kitchen.

"Hello, you two," said Sally. "I hope you had a nice day. James told me you all went for a hike and afterwards, he left you off in the village to explore a bit on your own."

Brenda and Stevie looked at James, who gave a brief nod of his head. They replied in unison, "Yes, he did."

"And we found the most wonderful candy shop," Brenda continued. "We'll have to go back there again."

"Oh, yes," said Sally. "I do love it there. The smell alone adds nearly two stone whenever I visit. Oh sorry, dears," she said at their look of confusion. "Two stone is nearly thirty pounds! Dinner will be in fifteen minutes," she added, and went back to the kitchen.

"Where is Mrs. Holmes?" Stevie whispered.

"She's out with that bumbling Constable," James said. "Something about the attack by and subsequent capture of the black panther. There's a great deal of disagreement about what was seen that night. Bobby's mum argued how the whole thing is being mishandled. She also said she was sorry to have to leave, and that Sally would take good care of you until she returns."

"Are we the first ones back?" asked Stevie.

"Yes," answered James. "Your mate Michael is upstairs, I believe. I saw him previously while taking some items up to the attic."

Bobby rushed through the front entrance and they turned his way.

"I'm glad you're all here," he said. "I have a lot to tell you."

"Hush," said James. "Let's go upstairs first." The group made their way up to Bobby's room and shut the door.

"Wait," said Stevie. "We need Michael."

"I'll get him," said James.

Bobby eased onto the bed and lay back, with his feet dangling over the side. Brenda poured herself a glass of water from the pitcher on the bedside table and told him where his mother had gone. Stevie plopped onto the floor, with his back to the wall, fished out a few round stones from his pocket to help him concentrate. All was quiet for the briefest of moments, as the trio gathered their thoughts and waited for Michael. Then the door flew open and James hurried into the room.

"He's not there," he announced with controlled anxiety. Bobby sat up with concern. Brenda, with a mouthful of water, swallowed slowly. Stevie stopped moving his stones and stared.

"What do you mean 'he's not there'?" asked Stevie.

"I mean that he's not there. I passed him not long ago as I was doing some chores. And now, he's simply not there."

"Dinner!" shouted Sally.

All three kids looked at each other.

"We've got to find him," said Brenda.

"Right," piped James. "But I'm the best one to do so. You three go down to the kitchen. Tell Sally I'm fetching Michael, who wandered off. I'll be there in a moment." Bobby nodded and they hurried downstairs.

They gave the message to Sally and took their places at the table.

Bobby knew there was a problem. He could feel it. Something wasn't right.

"What's wrong with you three?" asked Sally as she got dinner on the table. "You look so glum."

"Oh, we're just a little tired," answered Brenda. "We've had a busy day walking around the village." She didn't sound convincing, not even to herself.

The doors to the kitchen pushed open and James, looking troubled, entered the room.

Sally looked up with a smile, "Did you find him?"

"Uh, no, Miss Sally, I did not, but I do remember now, he mentioned something about going to meet up with his mates, earlier. I'm sorry I forgot. We'll have a quick bite and then the kids and I will take the car and go look for him."

They ate very little, very quickly and were ready to go in less than five minutes.

"You kids meet me out front. I'll get the car." James pushed himself away from the table and said to Sally, "We should be back soon."

Michael realized he had taken a wrong turn on his way to the village. He had been so preoccupied with his thoughts that he lost his way. He turned to look behind him. The growing darkness and rough terrain had obscured his footprints. Also, there were trails that crisscrossed each other. Did he turn right or left? Or did he go straight? He wasn't really sure at all. He looked around and saw that he was descending into a valley. If he turned around and got onto the left path that would eventually take him to the top of a small hill. Maybe that would allow him to see where he was and maybe even see Goathland.

Michael turned around. He followed the path to an intersection and turned left. The path led him up a knoll that now appeared smaller than the ones behind it. He climbed to the top and looked in all directions. The gusty wind chilled him to the bone.

He was not happy that he could not see Goathland from where he stood, nor did he hear any sound that would alert him of its whereabouts. He could hear nothing above the constant keening wind. He decided to move on. He kept going in the direction of the path he was on, which led him down one knoll and up another. He figured that if he stayed on a path, he would eventually come to someplace safe: maybe a farmhouse, or a cluster of homes, or even another small village.

"Stay calm," he cautioned himself, with his finger in the air. "My friends will come for me."

Bobby, Brenda and Stevie climbed into the car with James at the wheel. They headed for the village, hoping to see Michael along the way. It was easy to get lost, James knew, especially in the dark. There were too many footpaths to accommodate hikers and farmers alike. Some were old, while others were very old. Some led to farms, while others seemingly led nowhere, going on for kilometers without a smidgen of civilization in sight. To be lost on the moors at night would not be a good thing—not for anyone, even an experienced hiker.

They drove slowly through the village looking in every nook and cranny. Goathland was small so it didn't take long. The few shops that existed were already closing. They drove by slowly and saw nothing amiss. They soon passed the Me and Ewe Pub and proceeded out of the village proper. James slowed to a stop and pulled off to the side of the road.

"He's lost," said Bobby. "I knew it when we left the inn."

"I know," echoed James. "But we had to look."

"That settles it," said Stevie. "Let's get some gear and go look for him."

"Are you daft!" James roared. "You aren't doing any such thing. I'll be taking you back to the inn where you will stay put. I will then call Constable Wigglesby and organize a search party. Without you!"

"James," Bobby said softly, interrupting a no doubt feisty response from Stevie. "You know we all must go. Not only is Michael our friend, we have information the authorities simply wouldn't believe. They wouldn't know where to look or what to look for. If we told them what we know, or think we know, they'd ignore us and our request to search for Michael. Our friend is in danger, and we're the only ones who can help him."

James was frustrated. He knew Bobby was right about the lack of help. That pompous Constable Wigglesby wouldn't lift a finger until late tomorrow, anyway. By then it would be too late. He sighed heavily.

"You must convince me, then. Tell me what you know; I'll decide if we should proceed. And if you don't convince me that we have something that will lead us somewhere, I will call a halt to this foolishness and you will be locked in your rooms until morning. I will not have us traipsing about the countryside in the dark willy nilly. Is that clear?" They all nodded agreement.

Brenda told the group of her and Stevie's trip into the village, of meeting the old man on the bench and his advice to seek out the Travelers. She spoke of their visit to the candy shop and what the old woman told them.

"She said something about a caravan park near the town of Rosedale Abbey."

"I know the place," said James.

All eyes turned to Bobby.

"I can't share everything yet," said Bobby. "It's too long a story and some of it must be kept secret. But I am sure that we are up against a dangerous and vicious monster, unlike anything we could even imagine. I'm going to have to ask you to trust me for a while, because I'm also sure that we have less time than we think. So, we should go now and hurry. I agree with Brenda and Stevie that we'll know more when we get to the gypsy camp."

James was reluctantly convinced, mostly because he could feel Bobby's fear. Now that he had a destination, James turned the car around and headed back to the inn. On the way back, he laid out a plan. The kids were to stay in the car while he went in to explain to Sally that they were still looking for Michael. He would then call and leave word for Constable Wigglesby to organize a search party as soon as possible, knowing that nothing official would happen until morning. Lastly, he would tell Sally to lock the doors until they all returned.

He did all of that and when he got back in the car, James handed out individual, inexpensive torches, or flashlights, and bottles of water. He started the car and they sped off to the caravan park along the North Gill River, near Rosedale Abbey, and their rendezvous with the gypsy camp.

✝✝✝✝✝

Michael stumbled in the dark, fell and skinned his knee. He couldn't see the blood clearly, but he could feel it drip down his shin, and his knee hurt when he tried to walk. He decided to whistle while he walked, which his mom taught him to do whenever he got nervous, but he couldn't seem to make that happen. His lips wouldn't work and his body shook. From the cold, he told himself. He pushed ahead, sure that he would soon find his way to civilization.

He paused at a now familiar sound; the nervous bleating of a sheep. At least, that's what he thought it was. He listened again to be sure. And if there was a sheep, he reasoned, there must be a farm nearby. He moved towards the source of the sound. It took him down a hill and into a darkened valley.

The path turned to the right, went through a bundle of brush and opened into a small clearing. The moon cast a shadowy glow, as it continued to play hide and seek with the gathering clouds. The air was warmer here, protected from the wind by the surrounding hills. There was a sheep, Michael saw, with his front hooves caught in an exposed tree root, unable to free itself.

The sheep whined in fear and pain. Michael took a step in its direction to help, when a large, furry blur flashed by in the corner of his eye. The blur came from the trees, running on all fours until it jumped on the poor creature. Michael stood in shock, as the beast tore the sheep apart, eating voraciously. Bits of sheep went everywhere. Michael, initially stunned, could not stop looking at the horrid scene. He finally got control of himself and moved backwards slowly. He stepped on a dry twig, which, when it broke, sounded louder to him than a gunshot. He paused again, hoping it went unnoticed. It did not. The hungry monster glanced up at the sound and sniffed. He glared at Michael, grinning with impossibly long and bloody fangs.

Michael had never been this afraid in all of his life. Once, years ago, some mean kids had played a trick on him. They dared him to climb a water tower, telling him he would find a bag of candy at the top, and if he would go up and get it, they'd share the candy and let him hang out with them. Michael believed them and, despite his fear of heights, started the climb.

On the way up, the other boys shouted encouragement.

"You can do it," they screamed. "Keep going, you're almost there," they yelled. "We'll let you eat whatever you want," they added.

176

Michael didn't look down. He knew not to do that. But he did go very slowly, grabbing each step tightly, pulling himself up with care and placing his feet down on the thin bars one step at a time. He could hear them laughing below, but he thought they were laughing about the fact that he was getting closer, actually doing it. It seemed to take forever, but he finally reached the top and entered the walkway that circled the tower.

"Where's the candy," he shouted down, holding onto the waist high bar for dear life.

"There's no candy, you idiot," they shouted back at him. "Have fun getting yourself down."

The hurt Michael felt at being betrayed was almost as deep as the fear he felt looking over the railing. He couldn't take his eyes off the steep climb he would have to do in order to get down. He was petrified and found it difficult to move at all. He imagined himself falling to his death. It put him in a state of paralysis. Thoughts of his mother and how upset she would be at finding him, finally moved him into action. He slid under the cold iron rail and placed his feet on the first wrung. He took a quivering, tentative step, then followed with his other foot. He then gently lowered himself to the next wrung. He believed with all his heart that each succeeding step was the one that would lead him to the grave. Each movement wrapped him in fear so deep, he thought he would freeze in that spot until he let go and fell to the earth so very far below. The cold wind howled. His fingers were numb, he started to shake, and his legs felt like Jell-O. By the time he reached the ground, he didn't even realize he had done so, because his eyes were closed tight. When he opened them and saw that he had made it, he collapsed in exhaustion.

Even that experience was no match for the fear that now coursed through his veins.

Michael turned and ran. His finger was up and he shrieked for help. He ran as fast as his tired and injured legs could carry him, pushing his way through the bramble, running without clear direction, feeling only the compelling need to escape. He was able to scream for help but once, before the beast landed squarely on his back. Michael was knocked to the hard ground, the air kicked from his lungs. He lay in agonizing pain, a great weight pressing down on him.

And then all went black.

19

James knew the way to the caravan park, but there was no direct driving route to get there. He had to travel north before he could go west, and it was difficult to see in the dark, as it was a very cloudy night and no street lights to guide the way. Despite those difficulties, it took them only thirty minutes to arrive.

The parking area was dimly lit. James pulled his car up to the only other vehicles in the lot. They were parked near a wooden sign, with an arrow pointing to the river. It read: CAMPSITES, THIS WAY.

James told them all to take out their torches, then led his troupe down the cleared path towards the river.

"Torch is a stupid thing to call it," mumbled Stevie.

"Oh, and I suppose 'flashlight' is a better word? When the object in question doesn't flash, but maintains a steady beam of light, like a torch? Is that what you mean?" replied James, irritably.

"I can't help it if you Brits make up silly words for things that everybody in the world already knows as something else!" argued Stevie.

"Ugh!" sighed James and continued on, while Brenda and Bobby smiled at the exchange.

The footpath was carpeted with wood chips, softening their approach. After a few bends in the trail, they came upon some tall grass, about four feet in height, softly bending in the light breeze. It covered the ground to both the left and the right of the footpath, winding its way towards a campsite about sixty feet away, which was lit by a smoldering campfire. They could hear the river gurgling in the near distance, as it flowed to the Rosedale Abbey. James paused before continuing.

"I don't like this," he whispered. "It's too quiet. I have a bad feeling that's knocking on my head and it isn't going away."

"So do I, James," Bobby said. "But I'm not sure if it's about this place, or one we have yet to visit tonight. Right now, we have no choice but to move on. We should be careful, though."

The group moved forward at a snail's pace. They got half the distance to the campground when James held up his hands to stop. They all stood up straight. They saw four pitched tents, but no sign of life.

"Who goes there!" came a scream from the right side of the trail. Torches were shined in their faces and their hands went up to block the blinding light. Suddenly, a chorus of laughter surrounded them. The torches were lowered, and as their eyes adjusted, they came face to face with the boys Brenda and Stevie had met at the candy shop in Goathland.

"Bryan?" Brenda asked.

"Oh, great," mumbled Stevie.

"Yeah, it's me. What are you doing out here?"

"I might ask the same, as well as why you found it necessary to scare the life out of us," said James.

"Sorry, sir, my name is Bryan," he answered, extending a hand. "This here is William and Roland, who never say anything because I usually do all of the talking. We're out here camping, with Mr. Niles Wentworth, the local scout leader in Goathland."

"And where might he be?"

"He's out with some of the older campers at the moment, teaching them nighttime survival skills. We'll cover that next year, so we volunteered to stay back and watch the camp until they return."

"Aren't you frightened out here all alone?" asked Brenda.

"No, not really. We heard about that rogue panther on the loose through Mr. Wentworth and that it was recently killed. Besides, we've camped here in the past many times and a good fire will keep anything away," said Bryan, smiling at Brenda.

Stevie rolled his eyes.

"Look laddie," said James, "we're in a bit of a hurry. We're in search of a group of gypsies, that we are led to believe are camped in the area. Have you seen them?"

"Sure. They're not far from here actually. Why would you want them?"

"I'm afraid we cannot say."

Bryan looked suspicious. "Okay, we'll lead you to them."

"Oh no, you're..."

"Stevie!" said Brenda. "Let him speak."

"Look," said Bryan, "I'll leave Mr. Wentworth a note. I'll tell him I took my mates Snipe hunting. You won't be able to find the gypsy camp in the dark without us, anyway, since we know where it is, and we'll get you there in half the time. Right mates?"

Roland and William nodded agreement.

"Won't Mr. Wentworth try to ring you?" asked James.

"No, he doesn't believe in bringing a cellphone while camping, and you can't get service here anyway."

James thought for a minute, looked at Bobby and then responded.

"Okay, then. Write your note."

"You can't be serious," exclaimed Stevie.

James shot him a look and Bobby grabbed his arm. Stevie pulled away and stormed off, while Bryan got a notepad and a pen. He wrote his note, placed it on the leader's tent and headed out.

They followed the footpath on the other side of their campsite, which led them to the river. They crossed it at a narrow point by walking over a rickety wooden bridge.

"It's scary in the dark," whispered Brenda. "The moon has been hiding behind clouds all night and I can't see much without the flashlight."

"Here," said Bryan, "take my hand and I'll get you across."

Stevie, two steps behind, fumed.

Once on the other side, they proceeded in a northwest direction, hiking for about twenty minutes.

"I smell smoke," said Stevie.

One by one they all agreed. They were close. They proceeded more cautiously, now, eyes and ears wide open. Within minutes, they heard music and singing. Banjos, guitars and violins, mixed with harmonica and the sweet voices of happy people singing their hearts out. Illuminated by the campfire, their shadows danced along the sides of the colorful wagons, neatly arranged in a circular fashion. When the group reached the outskirts of the gypsy camp, the campers noticed them. The singing and music came to a gradual stop.

"Can I help you?" said a soft voice with a strange accent, from their left.

"Would you care to come in and sit by the fire," echoed a voice from the right.

"Wait just a moment," said James, holding up his hand and turning to his group. "You scouts need to return to your camp."

"No way, I..." Bryan stammered.

"Now listen," said James. "I appreciate that you led us here, but that's as far as it goes. We have a mission to accomplish tonight and it doesn't involve you. I won't be held responsible for you either, so you need to go back. I promise we'll look you up when all this is over."

Dismayed, Brian turned to Brenda. "You promise?"

"Sure," she said, "no worries."

Stevie kicked a clod of dirt and rolled his eyes, seething with anger he found difficult to suppress. Everyone watched as Bryan, William, and Roland waved goodbye and returned the way they came.

The kids were now caught somewhere between wondering if they were going to be safe and embarrassed for interrupting the festivities. They didn't know what to say or do next. James stepped forward.

"May we speak to the person in charge, please?"

After some muted discussion, they were led to the

largest caravan, which stood like a sentinel at one end of the campsite. There were two narrow steps at one end, which led up to a large, ornate door with odd, foreign writing carved into its façade.

"It's Romani," whispered James.

There was an oversized silver doorknob poking out of the right side of the door, and a silver door knocker hung in the middle.

Their guide reached up, picked up the knocker and gently slammed it twice against the striker. A gruff and gravelly voice shouted from within. "Enter." The guide used both hands to turn the knob and pulled the door open. It creaked loudly on rusty old hinges. The interior was dark, the darkness broken only by flickering candle light.

"Well," said James, "I suppose we should all go inside, then."

They looked at each other, wondering who would take the first step.

"Out of the way," said Stevie, still fuming, as he pushed his way through the small crowd and climbed the two steep steps to enter. Brenda quickly followed, then James and lastly Bobby, who was beginning to feel very weird about entering the caravan. "James," he whispered.

"I know, laddie, I feel the same."

The interior space was large and round, with room for about three or four abreast. It was also very deep, giving the appearance of looking down a long, wide tunnel. At the end of the caravan away from their point of entry, sat a small man in an oversized, stuffed armchair, creased from age, befitting its occupant. The only light source came from a few large candles that backlit the old man, making it appear as if his white, fuzzy hair was on fire. His image was further blurred by the corn cob pipe he was puffing, the smoke encircling his head like a halo, helping to obscure his features.

Stevie, Brenda and the others moved deep into the caravan, the door being shut for them from behind, making it darker still. They peered through the dim light towards their host. Bobby elbowed his way through, getting to the front of the group. He stared intently as the outline of the man's features slowly came into focus. The old man leaned forward and lit another candle, which lay on a small table set in front of him. He sat back and waved the smoke away, crossing his arms while chewing on the end of his pipe.

Bobby leaned forward not daring to blink, lest the man disappear before him. His eyes widened in surprise.

"You!" Bobby said.

20

Michael was alive, but in a great deal of pain. The agony came from everywhere. His head ached badly. It throbbed with a rhythmic pounding, as if someone waited every three seconds to hit the back of his skull with the heel of a shoe. His legs trembled, as if he'd been dragged on the ground behind a runaway horse. Even his eyelids hurt when he tried to open them, so he didn't. He wanted to know where he was, but he was afraid to look and actually find out. The last thing Michael saw still registered in his mind's eye and it frightened the daylights out of him.

He could hear several people murmuring. He couldn't decipher what they were saying because they spoke in a low voice, almost too low to hear. Whatever they said, they kept repeating it, over and over again. There seemed to be more than one person because someone was giggling while the others repeated a haunting chant.

It smelled badly where he was, too; disgusting, like the time the septic overflowed at his house. That was a *really bad* smell, Michael remembered, and he had refused to go outside until the man came to fix it. This foul smell, much like that one, had made him nauseous and he started to gag. He tried to stop himself, but a small choking sound slipped from his lips. He knew immediately that he was in trouble. He knew because the chanting stopped and he could almost feel the eyes that were now crawling over him.

"What shall we do?" whispered Hestra. "Shall we eat him?" Michael began to shake uncontrollably, despite his efforts not to move.

"Oooo, wouldn't that be lovely, now," cooed Helga. "I wouldn't mind gnawing on that right leg there, myself."

Bertha giggled. "Stop it you two," she brayed. "You'll frighten the poor lad. He's not for us to eat, now is he? Nooo, it's not for our meal that we've saved him, isn't that right girls?" All three of them laughed and cackled through their broken teeth, their bodies shaking until their hoarse laughter came to an abrupt end.

Michael risked a peek, cracking his right eye open until it was a small slit. What he saw appeared strange and out of focus. There were three fuzzy blobs standing a few feet away, reeking of a putrid smell. There was something very strange about them. It wasn't until his sight cleared that Michael realized he was hanging upside down and staring at the blobs from their feet up. As he tucked his chin and looked upwards, Michael realized he was looking at people, such as they were. And they were staring back.

Michael's hands were tied together in front of him. He pointed his index finger and the three creatures in front of him immediately looked at the floor where he was pointing.

"Excuse me, please," Michael said. "Can someone help me get up? This is giving me a headache."

The three hags paused a moment, then burst into hysterical laughter, laughing so hard, they grabbed their sides and drooled down the front of their filthy tunics. Finally, Bertha nodded to Hestra, who retrieved a large sharp knife from a side pocket. She approached Michael who was trussed and hanging by his feet from the rafter above him. Michael closed his eyes again, thinking he was going to be pierced by the knife, but Hestra reached up and with a smooth swipe cut the rope that held his tied feet to the ceiling. Unseen by Michael, Helga had also approached, grabbing his tied hands and lifting upwards, so that when he fell, his feet, and not his head, hit the floor with a loud thump. The two then hoisted him up and shoved him into a hard, wooden chair, using fresh rope to secure his arms and legs to it. Michael gave no resistance, accepting his fate, too tired to do anything else.

"Now," said Bertha, "let's have some fun."

Bobby stared in amazement. He couldn't believe his eyes, but there could be no doubt. Sitting right in front of him was the old man who had issued him warnings about coming to the North York Moors. It was clearly the man in the train station tunnel when Bobby had first arrived in York, and the very same man who tried to warn him at the Dracula Experience in Whitby. Here he sat, in the head wagon of the gypsy camp, chewing on the end of a corncob pipe. And he was smiling.

"Hello my boy. My name is Belcher and I am the leader of this clan. We meet again, I see."

"Who...what...I should have seen..."

"Yes, you should have. Seen, that is. I know you have a special power. Both of you do, in fact; you and the short stocky man there," he added, pointing to James. "You are able to see things more clearly than others, because you have the gift. More people do than you'd realize. But you fight it a good deal of the time, don't you? You often doubt your instincts, when you should allow yourself to be carried along by the river that flows within you. I have it too, you see, although not as strongly as you. And because I do, I have some idea of what you are up against. The 'Sight', as I call it, does not allow one to predict exact outcomes in the future. It only allows us to see snapshots of it, pictures of what might be or even what might have been. We get a sense of things more acutely than others and draw inferences more intelligently because we can see such things. In other words, by warning us of possible danger, our ability allows us to make better judgments and reduce the risk of injury to ourselves and others. That is, if we use it properly."

"So, why did you warn me to stay away?" asked Bobby.

"As I have said, I know what you are up against. I have encountered the type of evil that exists here before, in other places, in other lands. And, I also knew you were coming. I had a vision of your arrival and the growing power of your gift, as did your enemies. There is a strong cosmic connection between all who share this talent, both good and evil. Those who would do you harm fear your growing power, but also want to get their hands on it."

Bobby could feel all eyes were now on him.

"These evil ones have sought you out, specifically. They crave your youth as well as the immense strength of your developing psychic power. They feel that if they can subdue you, your power will make them stronger yet."

"I have felt a strange pull since I arrived here," said Bobby, "but I tried to ignore it. Is that the evil power you keep talking about?"

"Yes, it is."

"You keep saying 'they' when you speak of the evil that exists here. Who are they?" piped James.

"Alas, this I cannot see clearly, although I have learned much about them over time. I know what they want, for example, but I do not know exactly where they are. Through magic spells, they keep their position well hidden. I do know that they are close. And deadly."

"So, do you know of the monster of the moors that comes from an ancient evil?" asked Bobby.

The others looked at him. Bobby turned to them. "It's some of what I haven't been able to tell you yet, some of what I learned at the library."

"Yes," said the old man. "I do. And these others, the ones of which I speak, I also know that they control this creature and that he is deadly. He is a fiend that preys on the flesh of others. Half animal, half man, the beast does their bidding each night. But when the moon is full, he can turn others into what he is himself: a vicious wolf-like monster that kills to feast. It is difficult to kill such a creature and only silver will hurt him. We, my people and I, listen closely to the dark rumors that are whispered on the wind in many lands, and we have learned much over the years."

"I'll bet it's that butthead from the pub, that guy we chased in Whitby," whispered Stevie to Brenda, absently fingering the stones in his pocket. "He's the guy that knocked out Bobby up in that graveyard, and he's the guy with the wolf tattoo. It has to be him!"

"I'm inclined to agree with you, which, in itself, frightens me," added James in a hushed tone, as Bobby continued to address the old man.

"You said you don't know 'exactly' where this beast is or who his controllers are. Do you have a clue? A possibility? Anything at all that could help us locate our missing friend?"

"Your quest should take you to the Priory at Rosedale. Many of the whispers we have heard point there. It is a place that used to house Cistercian nuns. It has been empty for hundreds of years, but has recently been rebuilt. I sense a powerful force coming from it, and my people have heard of strange goings on recently. My intuition tells me it is prudent to flee, as death hangs heavy in the air this night. Therefore, I must tell you that my people and I will be leaving before dawn tomorrow, and I caution you one last time to do the same."

"What?" they all said at once.

"You mean you won't help us?" asked James.

"I have helped you," said the old man, calmly. "But

beyond this I can do no more. I warned you away, while trying not to draw the attention of the evil force that hangs over this land like a morning mist. Those forces are getting stronger. I have taken a great risk by allowing you to come to our camp to warn you one final time. I now must lead my people away to a safer place. And finding a safe place is always a challenge, as there are more wicked things in this world than you can imagine," he said, staring at Bobby.

"There must be," piped Stevie. "This is our second summer in a row for meeting a 'wicked thing.'"

They all stood silently, the spoken words of the old man draping them in a shower of fear.

"One of our mates is still missing and in grave danger," Bobby softly said. "And we're not going anywhere without him."

"I understand the bonds of friendship and admire you all for your bravery," said the old man, who began to unfurl a yellowed and wrinkled map. "So, let me show you the path to the Priory of Rosedale."

✛✛✛✛✛

Earlier, Wigglesby had raced back to the Wolf's Head Inn, but it was dark by the time he pulled into the driveway. Melanie practically leaped from the car, molded paw print in hand, muttering, "I'll be in touch," as she raced to the front door. Wigglesby was only too happy to spin out of the drive and head for home.

Melanie pushed open the large door, entered the inn, and was met with a wall of silence. There were a few lights on throughout the main floor, but the place was hushed, with no sign of life anywhere.

"Sally?" she called, her hollow voice echoing off the deadened walls.

A clock chimed on the half hour and made her jump.

"You're just being silly," she said aloud to herself, but simultaneously reached into her purse for her revolver. Melanie approached the kitchen swing doors, gently cracked them open and peered inside. She listened for any odd noise that would indicate a problem. She saw and heard nothing.

"Sally, are you home?" she called again, subconsciously frightened to raise her voice.

Gently, she nudged her gun between the two doors and pushed one of them all the way open. She followed her pistol into the room. She scanned the area again and flicked on the kitchen lights. They immediately chased away the shadows and most of her fears. Nothing looked or sounded remotely suspicious to her trained eye, so she returned to the lobby.

Placing her gun back into her purse, Melanie saw a scribbled note resting on the secretary desk, near the entry to the kitchen. She reached over and read it carefully:

Dear Melanie, James, and kids,
I called a friend of mine and went to pick up some food at the market. It will be quite dark when I get back, as it is not close, but I'll be home as soon as I can. Melanie, James and the kids went out to pick up Michael, who went for a walk.
Sally

194

Melanie sighed and placed the note back on the counter. She withdrew a pen from her purse and added to the note:

Everyone,
I've gone to York with some important evidence that I must test in our labs there. It is critical that I do this and I won't be home until early morning. Please stay indoors and be safe until I return. James, thank you for looking after the children.
Melanie

21

"Before you embark on your quest," said the leader of the gypsies, as he rolled his map back up, "I have something for you."

Belcher reached into a knapsack and brought forward a small pouch. He handed it to Bobby.

"It feels like sand," said Bobby.

"It is a very special powder," Belcher said. "It offers a unique and powerful spell. Once it touches the ground, it will prevent anyone from crossing over it. But be warned, it will take ten minutes before the spell begins and it will only last an hour. Therefore, you must be very judicious in its use. You mustn't lose it or waste it. It could, at some point, save your life."

"Thank you, Belcher, but…"

"Wait, there is more. Take these," Belcher said, handing Bobby two small stick like items. "These fireworks are very powerful, and I feel they will also be of value to you."

"How will I know how or when to use any of this?" Bobby asked.

"I'm not sure, my friend. That, you will have to decide. The time will present itself and then you will know."

"Well, gee, that narrows it down," whispered Stevie, drawing a stare from Brenda.

"And you," the old man said, turning to Stevie, "please take these and keep them. I feel strongly that they may be of some use to you." He handed Stevie a small pouch. Stevie, surprised at the unexpected gift, which felt like a bag full of marbles, put it in his left pocket until he could examine it later.

Bobby put the powder in his pocket and stashed the two Roman candles, tucking one into each sock and shoe, so they were out of site but hugging his legs for support and easy access. He shifted his weight and bowed his head, staring at the floor, the weight of the unknown wearing greatly on him.

James spoke for the group. "Thank you, Belcher. It has indeed been a pleasure. Thank you for all of your assistance and advice, and we all wish you and your people safe travels."

As they left the gypsy camp, Bobby led the way, following the directions Belcher had provided. They walked along the North Gill River towards Rosedale and the Cistercian Priory. The evening remained cool under a full moon that darted from cloud to cloud, dotting their path with dappled white light. The penetrating wind brushed along the river's edge, chilling any exposed skin. A chorus of frogs croaked in unison, until Bobby and his mates trudged too close. They then sat silently on their half-submerged logs watching the parade of would-be rescuers go by quietly.

No one spoke.

The building they sought in Rosedale was an ancient one, founded by an order of Cistercian nuns, a sect that for hundreds of years through the Middle Ages, was dedicated to a simple life of religious worship and hard work. The Priory, or building where they lived, fell apart in the 16th century. From then until modern times, only skeletal ruins remained of this former sanctuary against the evils of the world. It was not without controversy that those remains were secretly purchased and renovated by a new owner who was, himself, a mystery. This recluse would sneak about only under cover of darkness. He rarely, if ever, was seen in daylight, and only then like a ghost in the corner of one's vision, or the filmy substance of a fading memory. He had never interacted with the locals, until all but the most persistent observers lost interest and pretended to ignore him. He was viewed as a dangerous oddity, this stranger, and people spoke of him now only in soft voices, ever fearful of being overheard.

Such murmurs were carried on the wind and heard only by those trained to listen for them; people such as the gypsies encamped along the North Gill. People who are persecuted tend to be more alert to any menacing presence around them. They pay attention to the odd rumor, listen for the fevered gossip, and look closely for the concrete signs of slowly growing violence. The gypsies knew how to read the roadmap of danger, so when it became clear that a deadly force was near, they decided it was time to seek a safer refuge and flee this evil place. Although they could not have articulated it, none of that was lost on Bobby and his mates as they approached the outskirts of Rosedale.

It took them slightly more than an hour of rapid but contemplative hiking to reach their destination. The newly rebuilt priory stood ominously at the end of a dirt path, not far from the local church. It seemed sacrilegious, having a church, a home for the religious, so near what the locals now regarded as a bastion of evil. When they reached the edge of the sleepy village, they approached their target with a cloak of apprehension. They strained to listen for movement in the still air, hearing only their labored breathing and plodding steps. They made their way to the village church, its dark windows watching them like the black oily eyes of a giant ogre. They paused as one. Nothing moved in the dark. They dared not turn on their torches out of fear of being seen on approach. They had no idea what to expect but decided that a stealthy advance would be the best way to proceed.

Bobby stumbled and grabbed a nearby streetlamp for support. The others stopped and looked concerned, as they noticed that Bobby wasn't himself.

"What's wrong, laddie?" said James.

"My head," said Bobby. "It hurts. I'm getting a very strong message but it's all jumbled up. Nothing seems clear."

"I'm not feeling anything," said James. "I don't always, mind you, but often enough. Just not here and now."

"Are you okay to move, Bobby?" asked Brenda.

"No, not yet. My head is pounding. I need to sit down. Remember last year, Brenda? When we were at the tent of Madame Tarot and my head hurt so badly? This is worse."

"Sit down on that wall and rest, Bobby," said Stevie. "We've got this," he said with a great deal of forced bravado to impress Brenda.

"Here's what we'll do." James took charge. "We three will advance on the priory. We'll examine it from a distance, just beyond that newly built wall that encircles it."

"You, Bobby," he continued, "will remain here. Try to relax until you feel better. We'll come back and tell you what we see before we devise a plan to get closer, I promise." Bobby nodded his aching head and sat on the short knee wall near the church.

James, Brenda, and Stevie walked down the dirt path that skirted the church, towards the refurbished turret, the only visible remains of the ancient priory. If rumors were to be believed, it was the dwelling of the beast they sought. Or perhaps it was home to the evil that controlled the beast, spoken of by the leader of the gypsies. Maybe they'd even find Michael here—that was the thought that spurred them on, into the face of unknown danger.

"Do you see that?" murmured Stevie, as they rounded the bend and the structure became more visible.

"Yes," replied Brenda.

"It seems someone's home," whispered James. "I can see candle lights licking the interior walls. See there?" They moved towards the front gate, eyes darting everywhere, looking for cameras, warning devices, or any other signs of habitation.

"My heart is pounding," said James.

"No worries, old chum," said Stevie, patting James on the shoulder. "I've got your back."

James turned slowly to face Stevie. Stevie had a horse's grin from ear to ear, and Brenda held her face she was giggling so hard.

"What?" said Stevie. "You told me to never call you 'my good man' again, so I thought this would be better." James shook his head.

"It isn't," he said and turned back to the Priory. "There's not much to hide behind, between here and the front gate," James continued. "We'll have to run to it one at a time. I'll go first, but you two count to ten before trotting over. Stevie, you go second, followed by Brenda." They each nodded in assent.

James looked left and right, listened intently for a second, then sprinted across an open patch of grass towards the front gate. It was a tall structure, bound between two sections of wall

201

that completely surrounded the priory. It appeared to be the only way in or out. He counted and listened but heard nothing. He looked back at Stevie and waved him on. Stevie sprinted over to James and crouched next to him. He glanced back to keep an eye on Brenda. She gave him a short wave. Stevie held his hand up for her to stay there, until he counted to ten, then waved her on. She was at his side in seconds, breathing rapidly.

"Now what?" she asked.

"I've been examining the gate," said James. "It appears to be quite strong and in one solid piece. I don't see any wires or cameras, nor any way to release the door. There doesn't seem to be a handle anywhere. Both the gate and the wall are about two meters in height, so we're not going to get much of a view inside the wall, I'm afraid."

"Hold still, my good— Never mind, just hold still," said Stevie." Stevie attempted to climb onto James' back, but James uttered, "Wait just a moment."

James recognized what Stevie was trying to do and braced himself with bent knees and hands against the outer wall. Stevie stepped onto James' left thigh, then hoisted himself onto his back, stood up and grabbed the top of the wall.

✜✜✜✜✜

Bobby placed his hands on his knees and raised himself up slowly. He had taught himself to take deep, slow breaths whenever this happened, which often helped him regain control.

"That was a bad one," he said to himself.

While his head pounded, Bobby couldn't concentrate. He knew he was getting a vision, but of what, he couldn't see.

Dozens of images flowed through his brain at a rapid pace. They were like negative snapshots of events yet to come, mostly dark pictures of fast-moving figures; figures that were almost unrecognizable. Some he could identify, most he could not. By their size and shape, he knew he was seeing James and his mates, as well as himself. They were all running. Away from or towards something, he couldn't tell.

There was another figure, though; tall, dark, mysterious. Dangerous? That figure was running also. Towards them? He looked angry, determined. Was it the beast? Was he chasing them through the forest? Bobby grabbed his temples, tried to concentrate.

Oh no, there was more. It was Michael and he wasn't well. He looked beaten, in a great deal of trouble. And he was surrounded by…what? There seemed to be other people, and they were laughing at him. Poor Michael. They were going to have to get to him soon; of that, Bobby was convinced.

Bobby stood up all the way and shook his head clear. Whatever lay in front of them in the Rosedale Priory, they had to face it immediately. He took a step in the direction his mates went earlier and heard a noise. Someone or something was behind him. He stopped mid-step and listened. Some leaves rustled, but it could have been the wind. He dared not call out to his friends. A loud call might draw attention to them all, and that wouldn't be good for any of them. Maybe it was just an overactive imagination. Maybe he hadn't really…but wait, there it was again! Enough, he decided. Bobby whirled around, ready to battle anyone or anything in his path. The wind whistled and some leaves dragged themselves across the loose stones, but he saw no one. Just as he turned to rejoin his mates, someone came out of nowhere and clamped a hand over his mouth.

✛✛✛✛✛

"What do you see, Stevie?" whispered Brenda.

Stevie peered over the top of the stonewall as he stood on James' back.

"The lawn looks like crap. It hasn't been mowed and it's covered with weeds." Stevie and Brenda both kept their voices low.

"What about the building?" she whispered.

"There's a small building attached to the castle, but inside the wall. The castle part has slits, like for shooting arrows. I've seen that in dozens of old movies. There're windows over the slits now, but they're all closed. The building looks like it's been fixed. My dad calls it 'pointing.' You make cement and use it to hold the rocks together."

"As fascinating as this lesson in home repair is," said James, "my back will not hold you forever. Do you see any sign of life?"

"Nah, just the candlelight. There seems to be only one door and that looks closed tight."

"Okay, down you come, then." Stevie hopped off James' back, onto the earth below.

"What are we going to do, James?" Brenda asked.

"I told Bobby we'd be back before we did anything else, so let's go and make sure he's okay before we decide what approach we'll take," James said, while stretching his back. Brenda and Stevie agreed. This time, all three scurried up the path together back towards the church. They rounded the bend and froze.

"Where is he?" yelped Stevie. "Where'd he go?"

J. M. Kelly

James ran to the front of the church and tried the front door.

"He's not in here, it's locked."

"Where was he when we last saw him?" asked Brenda.

"Over here!" yelled Stevie. They all gathered at the section of knee wall where Bobby had sat down.

"Look at this!" exclaimed Stevie.

"What is it lad?"

"Someone else was here. Look at the footprints. And it looks like there might have been a fight!" Stevie pointed to a large set of footprints that appeared to come up behind a smaller pair, then a mix-up of the two.

"Aye, it does."

"What does it mean?" asked Brenda.

"I'm not sure," said James.

"Well I am," said Stevie. "He was taken. And it has to do with that priority building."

"Priory," corrected Brenda.

"Whatever! I'm going back and bust in that door!"

Stevie turned and ran towards the priory gate. Brenda and James quickly followed, softly shouting out warnings to 'slow down.' When they caught up with him, Stevie was standing mute in front of the large, heavy gate.

"It's open," he said.

He took a few tentative steps towards the gate that now stood ajar. He pushed it and it creaked wider, allowing all three to walk through to yet another surprise.

"The front door," said Brenda. "Somebody opened that, too."

The trio stopped ten feet from the priory. The front door was nearly three meters tall and one and half wide. It was made of solid steel, with a shiny silver coating and no window.

"These entries didn't open by accident," said James.

Interior light spilled into the outside darkness, through the small front door gap. James, Brenda and Stevie all took a forward step at the same time. After the third step, Stevie reached out and gave the door a shove. It was heavy, but well-oiled and opened all the way. They stepped into the foyer.

"Wow," said Brenda, softly.

"Look at that staircase," said Stevie. "It winds around the inside walls all the way to the top."

"And look at that artwork," gushed James. "The walls are covered with it. This looks downright civilized, like a museum." James shook his head and rubbed his eyes. "Let's not forget why we're here, though," he added quickly.

A small doorway was etched into the rear section of wall. A meager amount of light was coming from it as well. They all noticed it and moved in that direction.

"Stay behind me," warned James. "I'm getting a bad feeling about this."

They crept in tandem towards the doorway. James balled his fists, Stevie pulled out one of the stones he kept in his right pocket and Brenda looked for something to use as a weapon. Finding nothing, she huddled behind the other two. They entered the room beyond that door together and were immediately stunned.

"What kept you so long?" said Bobby.

22

The trio entered the unexpectedly large room as if they were looking at a ghost. Bobby was sitting on one of two stuffed leather chairs, both of which flanked a fireplace fully aflame. Between the two chairs rested an authentic Persian rug of some value, the entire scene looking like two friends having a friendly chat in front of a warm fire in an expensive hotel.

In the other chair, sat the waiter from the Me and Ewe Pub.

"Do come in and make yourselves comfortable," the man said, pointing to an oversized leather sofa that faced the two chairs. "We have much to discuss and it begins with this," he said, pulling up his sleeve, revealing the tattoo on his forearm that read *Lupus Occisor.*

James, Brenda and Stevie stared. The man who they had identified as their enemy was inviting them to sit and chat. And he was with Bobby! Bobby looked at them and smiled.

"Please sit," he said, also pointing to the sofa.

They entered the room with a mixture of fear and curiosity. Bobby was clearly not in distress, nor at all fearful about this man. Yet, they remained wary. After all, he had been the one that placed Bobby into a state of unconsciousness at the Whitby Abbey; he had been the one snooping around the village of Goathland when the attacks on sheep and people began; and he had been the one they were warned of by Belcher, the leader of the gypsies. His behavior was not normal, was, in fact, highly suspicious, and, as far as they were concerned, he was not to be trusted. For all they knew, he might even be the 'monster on the moors' Bobby's mother talked about. Stevie stared intently at the stranger and had a firm grip on one of the stones in his pocket, carefully selected for throwing, should the need arise.

"I understand why you'd be distrustful and perhaps not want to be in the same room with me right now," he began.

"He's not what you think," Bobby interjected. "Let me start," Bobby requested of the stranger.

The man sat back, crossed his legs, folded his arms and sighed. "The floor, as they say, is yours," he said.

"I had a suspicion that this man was not evil, but rather an ally," began Bobby. "When he grabbed me outside of Whitby Abbey, I felt the fear and pain related to his struggle. I also sensed that he felt no anger towards me. My trip to the Goathland library confirmed what I thought to be true, but I haven't had time to share any of that with you until now. You do need to hear his personal story. It will explain everything."

By now the three on the sofa were leaning slightly forward, hanging on every word. The stranger uncrossed his legs and sat up straight. He looked at them each in turn and saw the determination that brought them this far in their quest. He knew he'd have to be honest and complete with them and decided to tell them his entire story.

"I am the last surviving member of the Order of *Lupus Occisor*. My name is Alex Corbet and I am a direct descendant of Peter Corbet, the first official Wolf Slayer under the rule of King Edward the First."

And so the stranger began his tale. He told them of his ancestor, Peter, and the discovery of the den of Super Wolves. He told them of Peter's pledge for himself and his descendants to rid the land of these monsters forever. He told them of his family's successes and failures over hundreds of years trying to achieve that goal, leading up to the present day, and his personal attempts to complete their mission.

At the end of his tale, he drew a deep breath. All were silent, stunned at what they heard, taking a few moments to process it all.

"What is this place?" asked Brenda, hesitantly.

"I am a very rich man. My family fortune has grown over the centuries, and it has been used in various ways in the fight against the monster wolves and those who control them. I have many homes in many countries, most built by my ancestors. This one, I had constructed to give me better proximity to the evil that lurks here in the moors. I am here infrequently and do not interact with the townspeople. The less they see me, the less they pry, I have found."

"Yeah," said Stevie, "about those 'controllers' you mention. Who are they really, and what do we need to do to defeat them?"

"The first thing you should know is that they are old; hundreds of years old. They are the substance of legend, as alive and dangerous today as they were in my ancestors' time. They come from a long line of evil creatures just like them."

"Sounds like my math teacher," said Stevie.

"You may jest," continued Alex Corbet, "but the proud and ruthless Vikings of old greatly feared their kind. There are stories, both written and spoken of for a thousand years, of the Sorceresses of which I speak. The Witches of Westerdale they were called. A lineage of magical hags, schooled in the dark arts, casting their evil spells upon the unwary."

"Yup, definitely my math teacher," Stevie added. Brenda elbowed him in the ribs.

"You claim these hags are hundreds of years old," said James. "How can that be?"

"They mastered the spell of immortality during the time of my ancestor, Peter. Centuries ago, they concocted an evil formula, which allowed them to continue on in life, becoming ever more wicked and ugly with the passage of time. To do so, they need to draw blood from the wolves they control, soon after the wolves kill a victim. It is the key ingredient in their magic elixir."

"How do we kill them?" asked James.

"Killing them can be difficult. In order to destroy the witches, their bodies must be burned, or we must kill the lone remaining wolf that nurtures them. Without him, they cannot last. You see, even though they can survive the ravages of time, the price they pay is that they cannot leave the confines of their cottage, which is why they are so anxious to increase their meager food supply by turning you all into the beasts that they can control. That way, they will provide themselves with an ample blood supply for a long time to come. We cannot allow that to happen."

"What?" Stevie yelped. "They want to turn us into a beast of some kind?"

"Yes. And that is why you must know everything you can to defeat them before you try. And," he added, "you must begin to trust me, for I am your only ally in this."

"Why haven't you defeated them yet?" asked Bobby.

"I have traveled throughout Europe for decades, eliminating their progeny with the help of some key allies. For hundreds of years, the wolves were plentiful here in England, and during that time they spread to many other countries. Packs of Super Wolves colonized throughout the continent, which kept their individual pack numbers low and avoided drawing too much suspicion to any one location. I have spent the last few years tracking what I think is the last of their kind, here, in England. If I am successful, I will accomplish what my ancestors have tried to do unsuccessfully for centuries."

"Who was that monk you were arguing with at the Whitby Abbey?" asked Brenda, remembering their encounter in the church. "I saw you when we were there."

"I went to him for information, but he is a priest who no longer believes in the evil I seek and the quest I have embraced. For centuries, my ancestors had worked with the Church. Those who resided in the churches, abbeys and priories across Europe, collected information from the travelers who stayed with them. The stories, rumors, and gossip they collected were often helpful in tracking down our adversaries. The monk you saw me with in Whitby is young, part of a new breed and he has doubts about my work. He was reluctant to share information that may have been helpful to me, thinking it was foolish to do so. It is a sign of our modern times not to recognize the existence of true evil."

"Two things," said Stevie, as a thought struck him. "Why were you a waiter, and what was the big idea of taping me to the toilet on that train."

"As a waiter, it is easy to pick up on rumor and gossip. I hoped to get information on the events surrounding Goathland. And my belated apologies for our encounter on the train," said Alex. "But we have little time to lick our wounds. If we have any hope of saving your friend, killing the witches and eliminating the Super Wolf scourge on this land, we are going to have to leave now. We have much ground to cover tonight!"

"What's the plan?" asked Bobby.

"We will leave by car and proceed immediately to the Red Lion Inn on Blakey Ridge. It is our point of entry into the section of the moors in which we need to travel, and therefore critical that we arrive there soon. The proprietor is a close friend. He'll provide us with any fresh information he has collected, and provisions we may need for our quest tonight. From there, we go by foot in the dark of night, north to Westerdale. It's our only hope to approach the crones who control the wolf. I'm hopeful they'll expect us by road travel, and not by a hiking trail under the threat of a full moon."

"You know where the home is?" asked Bobby, standing.

Alex Corbett paused and grew quiet. He knew they had to get moving, and he was anxious to go. But, he couldn't let Bobby and his mates leave without fully understanding the risks ahead.

"It appears and disappears in the clinging mist that rises from the damp moors. Those who have seen their dilapidated shack and entered the boundaries of their property, usually didn't live to talk about it. There are surviving legends, however, of wandering men who told stories of a floating cabin where monsters dwell. My friend at the Red Lion Inn may have further information helpful to our cause."

He looked at the motley crew that sat before him. "Even though hiking to their location is our best option, we run the risk that they will know we are coming," Alex added, stressing every word. "It is quite possible they will feel your presence, Bobby, and they will send their beast to find you. We are all in danger, of course... but you, Bobby," he said, "are in especially grave danger, as you are the main prize they seek."

23

With reluctant steps, the group made their way to the black Land Rover parked in the rear of the Priory. James sat in the front passenger seat, while Brenda sat behind the driver. Stevie sat next to her and Bobby plopped behind James. Alex slid behind the wheel and turned the key. The sport utility vehicle pulled away in a rising cloud of dust and fear. Alex, the steely-eyed driver, scanned the roadside, alert for any signs of disturbance along their path. The road crawled through the darkened hills, a winding black ribbon leading them towards an uncertain future.

"I'm scared," Brenda said.

"Me, too," replied Bobby.

Stevie, not wishing to show his fear, reached over and grabbed Brenda's hand. "You're going to be okay," he said to Brenda, squeezing her hand. "I...I mean we'll protect you."

Brenda smiled at Stevie and squeezed his hand back. It made him blush.

"How much longer to the Red Lion Inn?" James asked.

"Almost there," whispered Alex.

After a short drive, they pulled up to the entry. A carved lion rested on a pedestal near the entry, a visual reminder of the inn's namesake. They disembarked and filed into the cozy looking pub. Once inside, they adjusted to the dim lighting and glanced around. There were a handful of people seated at a scattering of tables, enjoying a warm ale and a warmer blaze alongside the glowing fireplace. The small bar was near the back of the room, a variety of pull handles standing at attention, reflecting the wide number of local brews available. They made their way under the low, heavily beamed ceiling to the proprietor who stood behind the bar waving them his way.

"Alex, old friend," he said, grasping the stranger's hand while casting the rest of their troupe a wary eye. "How are you?"

"I'm well." He had noticed the owner's glance towards his new mates and answered the unspoken question. "They're alright, Bill," he said. "They're with me."

The owner nodded. "Let's go to the back room, shall we?"

They passed through two heavy oak doors to a private party room near the rear of the pub. These were heavy doors, the kind used to keep memories and secrets confidential. They all sat at a sturdy round table and faced each other. The owner spoke in a low voice and addressed his comments to Alex.

"I've never questioned your mission or methods, Alex, but do you think it wise to bring children with you?"

"I cannot explain it all to you right now, but trust me, they are crucial to the success or failure of tonight's endeavor. And if we should fail, we are all in very deep danger."

"The people out there by the bar?" questioned James.

"Not to worry about them, they're paying customers, staying here at the inn for a couple of evenings. I've already warned them not to go out at night, telling them that we don't allow guests to wander about in the evening beyond our grounds. They had also heard of the recently shot panther in the area. That was enough to draw them indoors after the sun went down."

"What information can you share with us?" asked Alex.

The proprietor glanced at this unlikely group again, then proceeded.

"Right. I have heard things; frightening things from some of our hiker guests. Many of them claimed to have seen an old shack in the forest, appearing out of nowhere, sitting on the wavy horizon like a frightening mirage. Yet, as they approached, the structure would disappear; just vanish into thin air. When they got closer to where they saw the mirage, it felt as if they were wrapped in an ice-cold air pocket, like winter trapped in a hollow, and a deep, overriding fear would engulf them. When they regained their senses, they hightailed it out of there and ran as fast as they could back to the inn. They felt foolish when they reached the security of the pub, almost convincing themselves that what they had seen and felt had never happened at all, that it was a figment of their imagination. Deep inside they knew better."

"Were there any stories of a kid? A tall boy with short hair? Did they hear any calls for help when they saw the shack?" asked Bobby.

The owner looked at Bobby and the skepticism he had expressed earlier seemed to melt away. "No," he said softly. "No word of any kind concerning a boy, I'm afraid."

"What about location?" asked Alex.

"I have good news there. The hikers were clearly spooked and although it took careful questioning and a few ales to get them to reflect, nearly each of them was able to recall the whereabouts of the mirage when it appeared to them. I pinpointed each of those locations on the map here." He took out a topographical map and spread it before the group.

"See here," he said, pointing to a series of red x marks clustered around a forest grove. "Each of the sightings are near this clump of trees. I have the coordinates for each observation; they differ only slightly. You can eyeball the general area at a distance from the lookout behind the pub."

"The Red Lion sits on the highest point in the North York Moors," explained Alex. "Just out the rear entry is a small hill with an identifying marker at its summit. The view of the surrounding landscape is extraordinary."

"But it's night and getting darker," said James.

"Gee thanks, Captain Obvious," muttered Stevie while rolling his eyes. He drew a sharp look from James, but Bill, the owner, continued.

"Yes, that's true, but there's enough moonlight to observe the area in question. I daresay that with a GPS, you will be able to find your way to the spot where the hikers saw the floating shack, even in the dark."

"I'm afraid we don't have that kind of equipment," said James.

"I do. We carry it for the hikers and bikers that stay here throughout the year."

Alex followed Bill to a walk-in gear closet. When they came out, they carried a high-tech torch and GPS for each member of their group.

"What about these?" said Brenda, holding up the flashlight she already had.

"You won't need them," said Bill. "The ones I'll provide you with are Pelican 8060 high intensity torches, with an added strobe setting, a reach of over 300 meters, and a body coated in solid silver. Any animal at night will be distracted by a high intensity beam shone directly into the eyes, and a switch to the strobe setting is usually enough to confuse and disorient them. The solid silver shell will serve you well if you find yourself in close proximity to... well, I suspect you know already. Just don't hesitate to swing hard and hit what you swing at. It may be your only defense when the time comes. I'm also giving you each your own handheld GPS, in case you get separated. They are pre-programmed for the mirage destination based on my collected coordinates, as well as this building for your return."

The group nodded, gave their thanks and proceeded out the rear door. They saw the marker at the top of the hill and immediately ran to it. Despite the darkness that accompanies night, moonlight bathed the valleys south of Westerdale that spread out below them. Alex examined his GPS and looked at the group.

"Stay close and keep up," he shouted above the wind. "We mustn't lose any more time."

With his torchlight turned on, Alex ran down the hill, turned at the hiking path sign, and was soon swallowed by the surrounding fauna. James, Bobby, Brenda, and Stevie quickly followed.

Trudging along the hiking trails in daylight could often be difficult even for an experienced hiker. Running along them at night was nothing short of hazardous. They dodged ruts and roots, loose rocks and outcrops. Once in a while, someone would stumble and curse, right themselves and keep running. The moonlight helped, but only marginally. If they were walking, perhaps it wouldn't be so bad, but running as fast as possible along an uneven path in the dark was foolhardy at best. Yet, they continued at a rapid pace, for all knew the stakes. Michael needed them.

From a distance, when the trail broke free of overhanging trees and bush, one could see their group as a line of bobbing torches snaking their way along a sinewy path, like a glowworm in a dark cave. Despite the difficulties of the terrain, all members of the group

J. M. Kelly

kept up, following their leader with blind faith in the hopes he would get them to their destination safely. They didn't dare consider what horrors awaited them.

They were approximately halfway to the coordinates, having just walked along a high ridge with a steep cliff that looked down into a deep vale littered with sharp boulders. They walked into a clearing, covered in purple heather and paused.

"Have you noticed?" whispered Alex.

"Yes," said Bobby.

The others looked puzzled.

"There's no sound," said Bobby. "No insects, no small animals crawling through the brush, not even a slight wind to move the leaves."

They all remained motionless, listening for something, anything.

That's when they heard it; an ear-splitting, mind numbing scream that pierced the stillness of the night. They jumped at the suddenness of the sound.

"What was that?" whispered Brenda. No one answered for the moment.

"It is the worst of what we feared," said Alex. "The witches have sent their beast to find us. They will want us all, if possible, but for you, Bobby, they would do anything. Your power, your skill, your youth, your gift is what they seek. Stay close everyone, I have some tricks up my sleeve if he gets close, but do not hesitate to use your torch as a weapon to strike him. Don't forget, it's made of silver, the one element he fears. It burns him when he touches it. A blow will kill him. We'll move more slowly and try to be as quiet as possible. James, would you..."

"I'm on it, I'll pick up the rear, then, shall I?" said James, as he moved to the back of the line.

The group moved forward quickly, half bent, listening for signs of danger as their eyes darted from shadow to shadow. Their bodies were tense. A distinct smell of fear hung in the air. No one dared say a word, but they didn't have to. They were all on heightened alert, waiting for the inevitable to happen and trying to be prepared.

They weren't.

With a speed and suddenness that even caught Alex by surprise, the beast sprinted from the tall bush that surrounded them and hit Alex with an extended arm that would have taken the head off an ordinary person. Alex hit the ground and didn't move. The rest of the group screamed, taking prudent steps backwards. The beast rolled after hitting Alex and stood tall, facing them with a toothy grimace. Saliva dripped down his jaw in anticipation. His claws unfurled, exposing finger nails that were hideously long and sharp. The curved nails on his toes dug into the soft earth as he prepared to spring. He was even more frightening than they had imagined. He let out a roar that shook the earth.

"Get back, you foul creature!" James screamed.

James pushed his way to the front of the group and held his torch high, as if to club the monster. Bobby, Brenda, and Stevie stood behind him, also at the ready.

J. M. Kelly

The brute was undeterred. He reared his ugly head back and howled at the moon, sending chills deep into the bones of those facing him. James' initial bravado faded as the monster leaped. He knocked the torch from James' hand with the swat of his left arm and brought the right one across James' face with a swipe and scrape of his claw. James hit the ground with a hard thud and didn't move. Blood poured from the cuts on James' face as he lay unconscious on his back. The monster now turned to the three of them. His mouth, full of dirty, sharp, wet, teeth widened into a grin as he readied for the attack. His muscled, hairy, arms were spread wide, with claws flexed as he bent his knees for the final jump.

24

Bobby, Brenda, and Stevie stood motionless, rigid with fear, facing a nightmare—something they'd become if they were bitten—and they felt powerless to stop it. Stevie and Brenda raised their torches high in the hopes of striking an accurate blow. Bobby quickly turned on the strobe light. It confused the creature for a moment. It was enough of a moment, as suddenly, a shot rang out.

The creature howled in intense pain. He turned to see his attacker, then rapidly fled into the bush towards the cliff they had passed, in a panicked attempt to escape. Now standing in direct line of sight for Bobby, Brenda and Stevie stood Alex, bleeding from the head, with a smoking gun in hand. Alex rushed up to Bobby and his mates. "Is everyone alright?"

"We are, thanks," answered Bobby, "but James is not."

Alex knelt beside James and felt his pulse.

"He's alive but in shock. Quick, cover him with your jackets. I'll place this rock under his feet for proper blood circulation." Everyone took their coats off and draped them over James. Bobby folded and placed his beneath James' head.

"I'm going to take a quick look down the trail towards the ridge we walked, which is where the creature fled. I'll follow his blood trail as far as I can. I'm hopeful that he's mortally wounded."

"What did you shoot him with?" asked Stevie.

"A silver bullet. Wait here, I won't be long."

While Alex was gone, the others tried to make James as comfortable as possible. They removed any pebbles that lay near or under his body. Bobby and Stevie tilted James' body up on one side, while Brenda removed the stones.

"Whew," said Stevie. "James better cut down on the fish and chips, he's a little hard to lift."

"Stevie, don't be rude," said Brenda.

Alex reentered the clearing, slightly out of breath. "It looks like the beast ran right off the cliff in his panic and landed down into the vale. His body is spread-eagled on some nasty looking boulders down below. He looks dead, but is too far to shoot accurately from here, so I'll need to climb down there and make sure. I'll be as fast as I can, but you must wait here until I return. I'm afraid we'll then have to get James back to the Red Lion."

"But what about the witches? And Michael? Do you expect us to just leave him there?" blurted Stevie.

"I'm sorry," said Alex with obvious concern. "I truly am, but I have to make sure this beast is dead at long last, and James clearly needs medical help." He looked at their faces. "I promise we'll try again tomorrow." With that, Alex rose and raced down the path to climb

226

down the hill. "I'll be back as soon as possible," he shouted as he ran.

"No," Brenda started to say, but Bobby grabbed her arm.

"Let him go. It's going to take him a while to get down to the monster and then back up here again. We don't have that kind of time; or, rather, Michael doesn't. Here's how I see it. The monster is probably dead. And even though the witches soon will be, that still may not be enough time to help Michael. James will be safe enough if we leave him here until Alex returns. We need to go and rescue Michael if we want to ever see him again."

"He risked his life for me last year without a thought for his own safety," said Brenda. "I'm in."

She and Bobby looked at Stevie.

"What are we waiting for?"

Each one looked at their GPS and started to leave.

"Wait a second," said Stevie. He then leaned down and got next to James' ear.

"Get better, my good man," he whispered. "Please."

✝✝✝✝✝

Michael was forlorn. He felt miserable and abandoned. He hadn't yet given up entirely, but he was beginning to accept that his friends would never come for him. He believed they had no idea where he was or what had happened to him. At least, that's what those old witches kept telling him. They teased him and taunted him without end. They told him what was going to happen to him; that they were going to let the wolf bite him and make him roam the countryside hunting people for food, just like the wolf. They told him he would never see his friends, never leave, and he would have to stay with them forever doing whatever they told him to do.

They are ten times worse than the students in my old school, thought Michael. They didn't know any better when they had teased him, that's what his mom had said. But these old ladies should know better. They were just plain cruel. The thought of never seeing his mom or his friends again brought tears to the corner of his eyes.

"Excuse me, ma'am."

The three witches hunched over their concoctions and jerked their heads up.

"Oh, my," said Hestra. "He must be talking to you, Helga. I haven't been a ma'am in over four hundred years." The three cackled away until they caught their breath.

"No," said Michael. "I meant the other one. She seems to be the boss."

Martha giggled at that, but Helga and Hestra did not. Helga walked over to Michael and grabbed his jowls with her pointed and dirty fingernails.

"So, I don't look like I'm in charge, eh?" she said.

"No, not really," Michael blurted.

"And why don't I, then? My spells are better!" Martha looked at her while she worked on her potions and grunted. "And I often tell the wolf what we want him to do and he obeys me! So what is it, boy? I'm curious."

"Well," said Michael, "You might tell the wolf what to do, but the older, uglier one tells you what to do, so I just thought that she was the one in charge."

Helga and Hestra laughed, but Martha just stared at Michael. When her two evil allies stopped laughing, Martha walked slowly over to where Michael was sitting and leaned over him so her hooked and crooked nose was an inch from his. When she spoke, she spoke slowly, and sprayed his face with her foul and disgusting breath.

"You dare to speak of me that way, boy? You dare to insult me like that?" Martha then placed her long, sharp fingernail on Michael's forehead and drew a bloody line down the side of his cheek. Michael winced with the pain and felt a burning trail down the side of his face, as if he had a long, thin string of fever.

"Throw him in the pit and let him wait there for our wolf!" said Martha.

The two crones each grabbed Michael by the arm and effortlessly lifted him off the ground, chair included. They marched him out the wide, double screen door and into an outside area opened to the sky. They cut his bonds and wrapped their steel-like grip around his upper arm and stood him up on the precipice of a steep hole dug in the earth over three meters in depth, with a diameter of double that.

"You see that?" asked Hestra. "That's where he sometimes has his meals," she barked. "He tries to keep them alive for a time, so he can tease and torture them, before he devours them." Michael looked down and held his index finger high in the air.

"What are you pointing at, eh?" barked Helga, looking up at the sky.

"Yes, I see it," Michael responded. "But I don't like it."

To their surprise, Michael leaned slightly over the edge to get a better look. He stared intently at the dark cavity, noticing a collection of white objects strewn about the bottom. Just as he was about to ask what the objects were, the two hags pushed him forward and he toppled into the pit, pinwheeling to keep his balance. Michael landed on his feet but toppled over when he hit the bottom. His legs hurt from the jolt and he fell on his shoulder, injuring his right arm. He carefully picked himself up and dusted himself off. He heard the two old ladies laugh and cackle, as they retreated back into their shack. Michael stood up and looked around. It was dark, but in the corner of his eye, he could see things crawling about, disturbing the dirt underfoot and climbing up and over the scattered white objects. He bent over to examine one of the objects and decided to pick it up. It was round on one side and half-buried in the loose earth. Michael dug it out with his fingers and held it up to see it better. In his hand, he held the left half of a human skull, complete with a partial jaw and teeth.

He screamed and backed away as he dropped it to the ground.

no one to be responsible for but himself. But he felt something with this group. There was something special about them. He was going to have to trust in their ability to stay alive until he could get back and provide help. He took a last look at the direction they went, turned around to hoist James over his shoulder, and, using his GPS, took a path out of the area to a working roadway. It would be the fastest route back to the inn.

dim, as if filtered through thick motes of dust. The closer Bobby got to the end of the hall, the louder was the humming. It was an indecipherable tune, but one that appeared to have a specific purpose. Certain parts of the melody were emphasized over others and sung with an ominous conviction that was frightening. Bobby knew that the witches knew that he was here. *They couldn't have missed the slamming of the front door, he thought. They probably were the ones who slammed the door.*

Despite knowing that he was doing the right thing, Bobby was flat out scared. Now at the end of the hall, he lost some of his courage and had a powerful urge to retreat; to run back out through the front door and escape as fast as his legs would carry him. But again, he thought of Michael. Knowing that he was somewhere in this house made Bobby angry.

He swallowed his fear, took another step forward and rounded the corner. Suddenly the ugliest, most evil looking being he could have imagined stood right before him. Her hooked nose, stringy hair and foul odor stunned him, but her eyes, and the intense, evil look she fixed on him, froze him to his spot. He was so shocked by her looks, that he never heard the footsteps behind him, nor had the time to resist the viselike grip placed on both his arms.

The lack of sound was frightening enough, but not having any idea what was happening inside the house, drove Brenda and Stevie crazy. They remained huddled together at the edge of the clearing, staring at the mist enshrouded house, worried about the fate of their friends inside.

"I've had enough!" shouted Stevie.

"Wait," called Brenda, but she was too late. Stevie yanked his arm away from her and marched up to the front porch. Not really knowing what he was going to do next, he stopped at the bottom step. Brenda crept up beside him.

"Stevie," she whispered. "What the heck?"

Stevie chewed the inside of his cheek and furrowed his brow. It took him a second to decide and another second to act. He reached into his right pocket, retrieved a round stone and fired it through one of the two windows that flanked the front door. It barely registered a noise, as it cleanly pierced the pane, sending the stone into the depths of the battered shack. A loud shriek cut through the silence as the projectile hit someone in the bowels of the house. Stevie looked at Brenda.

"Oh crap," he shouted.

They ran back to the edge of the clearing and ducked below some tall shrubs.

"What were you thinking," scolded Brenda.

"It seemed like a good idea at the time."

What happened next resembled a nightmare. The front door flew open and hit the interior of the house with a loud bang. A plume of dark smoke poured out, and when it cleared, there stood a horrific looking witch with the yellow eyes of a cat. Her parted mouth had spread earlier. Both groups stared at each other, each wondering what the next few seconds would hold.

Martha lifted her hand, accepting her fate as waves of hot air poured over her and her sisters and pointed an accusatory finger at Bobby.

"The world is not through with you yet, boy," she shouted over the noise caused by the firestorm behind her. "Your power attracts many. We are not alone in noticing it, and you will not escape them all."

Stevie reached into his pocket and pulled out a round stone. Bobby grabbed his arm.

"It's not necessary, Stevie. Look."

Bobby pointed towards the witches' feet. All four of them were riveted, not really believing what their eyes were telling them. As the house burned down behind them, the witches were disintegrating into piles of dust and ash from the feet up.

"Their spirit must be in the house," said Bobby.

"It's being destroyed and so are they."

They continued to watch as the witches turned into a mound of black soot. Helga and Hestra wailed at their misery, not quite believing that their wicked time on earth was at an end, their cries echoing into the night even after they were gone. Martha continued to point at the foursome until there was nothing left but her extended finger, and then that too was gone with a gust of wind.

The fire continued to burn, lighting the night sky with its foulness.

"Let's go," said Bobby.

"Where?" asked Michael, his finger pointing upwards.

"I've set my GPS to take us back to the Red Lion Inn. That'll take us up to the road and we can hike from there. With any luck, a car will pass and perhaps give us a ride."

"At this hour?" questioned Stevie.

"Okay, a lot of luck."

They picked up their torches, turned as a group and ran along the path before them. Every now and then, Bobby glanced at his GPS and kept moving. Their lights bobbed through the bush, resembling fireflies in the summer night, until, at last, they reached the lonely road.

They looked north and south. Nothing but a dark strip of macadam greeted them, but it was a tangible touchstone of civilization and they could not have been happier to reach it. It reminded them of what was genuine and important in their lives, causing the memory of what just happened to fade like a horrible nightmare.

"This way," Bobby said, leading them to the right. They dragged themselves down the road with what little energy they had left. Their adrenalin was fading, along with the dwindling flames in the distance.

"I don't know if I can continue," said Brenda, stopping with her hands on her knees.

"We have to," said Bobby. "Come on."

Stevie put her arm around his shoulder and said, "Lean on me, Bren. I'll help."

She smiled at him, then shouted, "Look!"

"You don't understand," said James. "I had them on every door and window. They were a safety barrier. A protection!"

"A protection? Against what?" whispered Stevie.

They heard a loud crash upstairs; the sound of glass breaking into a thousand little pieces. Then a loud thump, like something being thrown across the room and hitting the wall. Footsteps ensued. Not the soft padding of an ordinary person scuffling down the hallway in their bedroom slippers, but loud, scratchy sounds, as if sharp nails were being dragged along the wood flooring, or a broken needle had skipped across an old record album.

"Maybe it's Sally?" asked Brenda and took a step towards the stairway.

"It isn't Sally," Bobby said, as he reached out and stopped her with his arm.

They all heard the breathing next. A hoarse, deep, guttural sound that sent fear coursing through their overtired bodies. Without thinking, they took a step backwards towards the front door. They paused when they heard someone moan. Across the room, in a far corner, lay Sally, next to an upturned chair. James rushed across the lobby to get to her.

"She's been hit and knocked unconscious. She's bleeding, too."

The others heard him, but couldn't speak, their eyes were glued to the stairway and the dark space at the top of the stairs. The scratching got louder. The breathing morphed into a raspy, wet, low growl that paralyzed them. All of them, including James, who knelt down and cradled Sally, could not remove their eyes from the spot at the top of the stairs.

They saw his long, muscular arms first, in the dim light of the lobby, with those grotesque long-nailed fingers that clawed the side walls as he walked. Next, his hairy, massive chest emerged from the shadows, a bloody mess from the gunshot earlier. Then, his long, dripping snout, full of sharp and dirty teeth. He snarled, sending shivers down their spines. They were frozen with fear and unable to move.

They thought they had seen the worst, but then they saw his eyes. They were red and yellow in color, like the bloody orbs of an ancient predator. To look directly into them was to gaze into your own painful death.

"We'll never get away," Brenda cried.

Bobby looked around to no avail, realizing they had left their gear in the car. There was nothing he or anyone could do. Even if one of them made it to the front door, they'd never outrun the creature.

The beast flexed his claws, extended his arms and opened his jaw. He grinned with those wet, ferocious fangs, and paused halfway down the stairs, letting fear course through his victims. He could hear their hearts beating rapidly and it made him smile.

Unaware that he was even doing so, Stevie reached into his right pocket, but found it empty. A subconscious thought tugged at his brain; a memory of something he was supposed to recall. His brain, now on autopilot, kicked in, and the thought surfaced. His left hand reached into his left pocket and came out

"Me? Of course I didn't take it. See here, I've had enough of this nonsense. I'm leaving. I'll be stopping in to see Ms. Jenkins in hospital, then I'll be returning to my office to file my report. I can assure you that with the rogue panther caught and a lone, long gone burglar to investigate, along with careless, missing children and dead sheep, I've had about enough of Goathland for the present. Good day, Ms. Holmes."

Perplexed, Melanie was left to wonder what really had happened in her absence, as well as what happened to her paw print and lab report.

Bobby's friends had three more days before they had to leave for home. They spent them hiking the countryside, exploring the town together and going for car rides through the North York Moors Park with James, who had recovered his car. Those three days went by swiftly and they suddenly found themselves having to say goodbye. Bobby accompanied them to the airport, as James drove. The ride was a quiet one. It was hard to create idle conversation around so much of what you wanted to forget. In silence, however, they were able to make peace with their shared experience, despite its lingering violence.

Once at the airport, they could not let each other go without saying farewell.

"Remember," Bobby said. "We can't speak of this to anyone but each other." A group hug, that included

James, sealed the deal and the three Americans walked to security, with shouts of promises to email.

James swore he heard a familiar voice howl, "Take care, my good man."

Bobby and his mum planned to leave the next morning. Bobby was up early and said he was going for a short walk into Goathland and would be back soon. On his way, he snuck into the inn's garage, retrieved a brown bag that was hidden under a table, and went for his walk. He took in the fresh air, even though it was tainted a bit from the lambs that wandered freely. Watching where he stepped had become second nature to him by now. He liked the small village atmosphere, the friendliness of the people and the beauty of the countryside. Knowing that an ancient evil had been eliminated, and that he and his mates had played a part in that, made him happy. He paused in front of a familiar building, went up to the door and entered.

Later that morning, Mr. Patrick O'Reilly opened the downstairs door to the library. He climbed the interior staircase to unlock the entry to the library and saw a brown paper bag sitting on the landing in front of the door. He took the bag inside and removed its contents. He was amazed to have such a treasure. There was a note attached. It read:

Dear Mr. O'Reilly,
Here is your proof. Now, go and convince them.
Best of luck,
BH

Melanie had contacted her office in York several times over the course of several days, attempting to retrieve another copy of the missing report and possibly another sample of the paw print that went missing. She was eventually told by her superiors that the matter was now deemed highly classified and taken over by another branch of government. Therefore, the matter was effectively closed, she was sworn to secrecy and not to speak of it again to anyone.

On the way to London by train, Bobby sat in quiet contemplation. He stared out the window, letting his mind wander over what had happened, trying to come to terms with it. It would take time, he knew, and he had much to consider. He also knew that time and distance would help.

But in the back of his mind an echo would not leave him in peace. *There's more evil in this world than you can imagine, the Gypsy King had said. The world is not through with you yet, boy,* the witch had said. Would he have to face more evil? Would he and his friends ever be safe? He had no idea, but the prospects frightened him.

"Penny for your thoughts?" said his mum.

Bobby looked at her, tongue twisted, not quite sure how to express his fears.

"None of that story James told was true, was it Bobby?"

A loud silence sat between them.

"It's alright, son. I understand that there are times when you can't share your thoughts. I know you and your mates wouldn't be mixed up in anything too bad. As long as everyone is okay, I guess I'll let it pass. For now. But I want you to know that the time will come when you need to trust me and to tell me everything. And I want you to know that I'm here to help you." She reached over and grabbed his hand. "I'm always here to help you."

Seven months later, Bobby was bringing in the mail when he spied a postcard from New Zealand. It was a typical postcard sporting a variety of scenic images of a beautiful country. It would be the kind of thing that any traveler might send home to family, to let them know the person who sent it was having a good time. Bobby flipped the card over. His head tingled and his head began to hurt so bad he dropped whatever other mail he was carrying. On the card Bobby read just three words followed by someone's initials: ROTORUA-ATI-AWHINA, AC.

About the Author

J.M. Kelly has been a middle school teacher, a vice-principal, a principal, a Co-Director of the New Jersey State History Fair, a consultant for the New Jersey Foundation for Educational Administration, a current Board member of the Global Learning Project (a non-profit) and Past-President of the Morris County Association of Elementary and Middle School Administrators. He has been the recipient of numerous education awards such as the New Jersey Governor's Teacher Award, two Geraldine Dodge Foundation Grants, and by acclamation of his school staff, received the New Jersey Principal's and Supervisor's Association Principal of the Year Award for Visionary Leadership in 2007. He has authored two professional books: *Student–Centered Teaching for Increased Participation* and *In Search of Leadership*.

The Lost Treasure is his first novel. His love of mysteries, adventures and everything about Sherlock Holmes, helped in the creation of Bobby Holmes and his cousin Brenda Watson. *Monster on the Moors* involves the same characters in a pulse pounding thriller that takes place in the North York Moors of England. *Tommy Ails: Good For What Ails You*, is a humorous off-beat mystery, and his first novel for adults.

Jim's non-fiction book, *In Search of Leadership*, or *Sailing With Roland* takes him to the Maine coast and aboard the sailing craft of one of the most preeminent educators of our time, Roland Barth, to discuss educational leadership in particular and the field of education in general. The results are, what Roland in the Foreword calls, "timeless nuggets of wisdom for himself and for the rest of us who would venture aboard a boat and into a schoolhouse."

Jim divides his time between Sea Girt, New Jersey and Sarasota, Florida, with his wife Bronwen. They have three children.